Antipsychotic

Antipsychotic

LeAnne Hart

A Journey Written Through
Caffeine, Consciousness, and
Crashouts

Amegreen Publishing, LLC

To request permissions, contact the publisher at r.leanne@leannehartauthor.info.

Hardcover ISBN: 979-8-9986436-2-0

First Edition February 2026

Cover Art & Typography by LeAnne Hart

Printed by IngramSpark in the USA.

Amegreen Publishing, LLC
San Tan Valley, AZ 85149

Content Warning - Reader Beware

This book contains foul language and themes that some could find inappropriate, uncomfortable, or difficult to read, including abuse of multiple varieties, self-loathing, self-harm, death, suicide, stalking, sexual scenarios, religious/spiritual and political viewpoints, and the full spectrum of human emotion. If you are under 18 years of age or any of these things will negatively affect you, please stop right here and put this book down. You can always return when you are ready to have your mind expanded.

Dedication & Acknowledgements

I do not look for approval from any known source - I gave up on that idea when I was still young enough to crave it, but old enough to know that the world will never allow you to be as you wish. You're never skinny enough, or you're unhealthy. You're never talented enough, or you're overqualified. You're never smart enough, or you're too intelligent for your own good. You're never confident enough, or you're arrogant. You're a prude, or you're a slut. The list is unyielding and never-ending.

What frustrates me is there are souls who have become so jaded by others' opinions that their only release from those chains is the fleeting elation they feel from picking other people apart piece by piece. A monster created by an inability to truly see themselves, flaws and all, understanding that each little detail makes them the beautiful, unique piece of art that they are. I feel sorry for these people. They will never know what inner peace truly is. They will never see the world for its beautiful imperfections...they will always find what is wrong with the world, put it all on one plate, pick at it, analyze it, and create a dish of disappointing flavors.

I am exactly who I choose to be, regardless of whether you like it, agree with, or absolutely loathe it. I make no excuses or apologies for it. I will not be party to judge and jury by someone who doesn't even know my name, much less someone who has no idea of how I came to be. If you don't like it, the solution is simple...walk away. I never asked you to stand there and look at me through eyes overflowing with judgement.

For those who know what it is to crave acceptance and be denied, to beg even one soul for a bit of compassion when every fiber of your being feels not good enough, to want a single person to recognize what you have to offer and praise you for it...know that at least one person thinks you're perfect; at least one person believes you have more to grace this world with than you could ever know; at least one person who doesn't know your name or your story, who has never seen you at your best or your worst, but who thinks that your mere presence is the difference between permanent darkness and clear blue skies. You are you, and that's all you should ever need to be.

This book is for you. Every word, every line, was carefully crafted through decades of loss, regret, pain, love, desire, elation, and all the experiences that have shaped who I am. Some of it may trigger you...as it should, as it is meant to. We learn from our triggers, we grow through facing them and reshaping them into boundaries. I hope that as you read each piece, it resonates with you in some way. I pray that as you walk alongside me in my journey, it reminds you that I also walk alongside you in yours. We are eternally connected, and I am grateful you are here.

I would like to take this opportunity to acknowledge the souls who have inspired and uplifted me in my 42 years of life, and without whom this book would not be possible.

First, to my Mother Tina, who was not only the vessel through which I arrived on this plane of existence, but who has stood beside me through so many trials and tribulations that I know you wished I did not have to experience. Even when we battled each other, even when I pushed every button and overstepped every boundary, you never gave up on me, never abandoned me like the men who expected me to be anything other than exactly who I am. I am absolutely the woman I have become thanks to your grace, love, support, discipline, and all the unrealized dreams you sacrificed for my benefit.

Next, to my Siblings - Anthony, Jareth, and Raquelle - what a beautiful gift each of you are to me. I learn something new from you every day and stand stronger in myself because I have all of you to look up to. Your hearts, your minds, and your souls are infinite sources of light when the darkness consumes me, and I am only alive today because each of you has saved me in ways you will never truly understand. You are my Cornerstones, and I can only hope that I have, in some small way, given back to you all the love and support you have bestowed upon me. And to my long-lost brother out there in the world, I hope one day we find each other, so I can complete the picture of you all in my heart and my life, filling the space where you are supposed to be standing.

Third, to my Soulmates - Stephanie, Tessa, Israel, Lynette, Martin, and Jenn - the moment I met each of you was a moment in which my life changed forever. I have been so blessed over the years to collect around me a group of unbelievable human beings who challenge me, believe in me, and never let me forget how powerful I am. Even though two of you now reside beyond the veil, I still feel you with me every single day. Each of you means more to me than I could possibly express and has loved me in ways I didn't always deserve. I don't know what kind of karmic energy allowed me to find you all in this life, but I will carry you into the next one with unyielding gratitude. Thank you all for being the kind of people I aspire to be, and for giving me the kind of love that spans universes and lifetimes.

Last, but certainly not least and in no particular order, to my Found Family - Auntie Jen, Alyssa, Emily, GM, Visk, Sab, Ash, F.L., Nikki, Ashe, Surf, Phin, Momma D, Uncle James, David, S.M., Mille, Timothy, Pedigo, Ethan, Roma, Amanda, Sorionson, and all of the other amazing souls on TikTok (there's too many to actually name!) - I never expected when I began this journey to being a published author that I would find such an incredible group of people to rally around me, especially not on an app that I had vehemently avoided for years! But each one of you came crashing into my world and gave me something I had never really had before - a community of authors, advocates, and wildly creative minds who truly understand my crazy brain and appreciate my particular brand of neurospicy. During a time of absolute upheaval in my life, each of you have given me your kindness, your support, your trust, and your light. What a truly beautiful thing to have stumbled upon when I needed it most. I would not have found the courage to publish this collection without the encouragement that each of you has provided. I hope you all know how unbelievably grateful I am for accepting me into your lives, and how much I love you all from the depths of my heart and the most distant corners of my soul. We rise together, always!

Table of Contents

A Journey Built on Trauma **Page 1**
- Shallow Graves Page 3
- Hypocritical Patriarch Page 4
- Laced With Lies Page 6
- Comfortless Existence Page 7
- A Common Tale Page 8
- Road Blocks Page 9
- Paper Wings Page 10
- Diligent Page 12
- The Uncertain Path Page 13
- The Violence I Crave Page 14
- Circle The Drain Page 15
- Jaded Dreams of an Un-Mother Page 16
- It Never Leaves Page 17
- Suicidal Page 18
- An Evening with Death Page 19

The Beauty of Love & Lust **Page 25**
- Before Page 27
- Beloved Page 28
- Instigator Page 29
- No Stranger to Pain Page 30
- Silent Assurance Page 31
- A Kingdom of Desire Page 32
- Formidable Page 33

Quiet Calm Page 34
Raptor Page 35
Just A Taste Page 36
Alice & Her Hatter Page 37
One Page 38
As You Wish Page 39
Chapters Page 40
Devil with an Angel's Smile Page 43
Unsatisfied Craving Page 44
Subjugation Page 45
Entice Page 46
Collide Page 47
As It Should Be Page 52
Ambivalent Fascination Page 53
All I Have to Give Page 54
Driftwood Page 55
Not Quite Needy Page 56
Forty Years & Counting Page 58

Heartbreak – Life's Greatest Teacher Page 61
And So It Goes Page 63
Artist Page 64
Playing With Boys Page 66
Cheater Page 68
Boxing Match Page 69
Disparagement Page 70
Bridge Burning Page 71
Untitled 3 Page 72
Junkie Page 73
Lovers Quarrel Page 74
Something Like Closure Page 75

Long Dead Lovers Page 77

Social Commentary & Criticisms Page 79
The P. I. C. Page 81
Detachment Page 83
Optimistic Fool Page 84
To Be a Girl Page 86
Calculated Madness Page 87
Intangible Page 88
Misconception Page 89
Empathy & Regret Page 90
Deadly Seduction Page 91
Fucked Page 93
Obedience Be Thy Name Page 95
Gilded Purgatory Page 97
Divinity Awakens Page 98

Shadow Work Page 101
Pressure Page 103
More Than Restless Page 104
Alibi Page 105
Faith Misplaced Page 106
Sometimes We Fail Page 107
Alive Page 108
Jigsaw Page 109
Self-Inflicted Page 110
The F Word Page 111
Avarice Page 112
Lunacy Page 113
Embrace & Endure Page 114
Moving Mountains Page 115

Such Is Life Page 116
And So, I Write Page 117

Aware & Enlightened **Page 119**
Dear Brother Page 121
Dear Sister Page 122
Unaffected Page 123
Fond Affinity Page 124
Identity Page 125
Resolute Page 126
She's Got A Way Page 128
I Am Contradiction Page 129
Gift & Curse Page 130
Tits & Ass Page 131
I Never Knew Page 132
Truth Reflected Page 133
Incongruous Page 134
Balance Page 135
The Undoing Page 136
Never Call Me Indifferent Page 137
Stretch Page 139
Resistance Page 140
Fear Page 142

The Last Taste – Short Story in Progress **Page 145**

A Journey Built on Trauma

No coddling here. We're diving right in. I was born into trauma, as many of us are, so what better way to begin this journey than with the broken pieces that define my past, and some of the hardest moments I was forced to rebuild myself through? Many of these poems were written at a young age, which I then reshaped and updated over the years as my vocabulary and understanding have evolved. There are some very heavy themes here, so make sure you're prepared. This section is proof that even the darkest chapters of life can be survived and used to fuel the fires of regeneration.

Shallow Graves

A cemetery of long dead moments
Topped with the soil of scars from many lessons learned
No matter how persistently I dig
I cannot reach the wood of these coffins

A mind rough and calloused
exhausted from the strain of uncovering my past
I had buried the pain deep
Covered the anguish with cheap, store-bought
imitations of strength and grace
I became exactly who the world wanted me to be
Hiding all signs of the fractured, heavy heart I carried

Now unable to retrieve those fleeting smiles lost within
the folds of a childhood nightmare
As if I created a different kind of monster
One who could swallow the history I have been running
from
I tore out those pages,
ripped them carelessly from my thoughts
Until nothing was left but an incomplete puzzle of the
girl I once knew

The thought of finding those missing pieces, of
completing that picture
terrifies me
Do I really want to remember?
To once again hear the cries escape my soul?
To reapply the bruises fresh upon my psyche?
Or am I content to live the lie
I have, for so long, been content to live?
Just more answers I don't desire
to questions I fear to ask

Hypocritical Patriarch

Just couldn't be the adult, could you?

Didn't have the balls to be a man
to be accountable for the choices you made with that prick between your legs

Sure, leave it up to the little girl
who was never even aware of your existence
because you'd written her off before she even came into this world

She'd have been happier without ever finding out the truth
It wasn't even her choice to make
It's never been her choice to make
Another asshole made that decision for her
Another so-called man who didn't know the first thing about her

He never really tried
You never really tried
As soon as it became apparent
that she'd never be what you expected
You did what you all do best
You bailed
Checked out
Tossed her aside for those who don't share your blood
when she's the only one who shares your blood

You fucking child
You were all children
Forced her to swallow your perceptions
and created a monster out of her longing

for the one thing she had always wanted
You all made her this way
and now you chastise who she's become

How can you even look at yourself,
knowing you created so many scars on the surface of so fragile a heart?

And you call yourself a father...

Laced With Lies

Used...
As usual, become the crutch
Defend those who don't deserve atonement
Help those who don't appreciate the aide,
Never expecting anything in return...

The strong one, the smart one, the honest one
Outstretched hands filled with anger and pain
rely on a pile of broken pieces to be their Savior

Beg for relief
from the depths in which you've buried yourself
And asked to stand in waiting...
For what?
For a refusal to give back?
Turning falsity into a mask
Securing the feeling of deserving less
Even when the opposite is clearly the case

The anchor, the backbone, the cornerstone
For those who should be able to stand alone
and rapidly losing faith in the reason

Why continue fighting?
Is the risk really worth the reward?
What even is the reward?
No longer wanting to be the superhero, the saint
So weak under the crushing weight
And yet, continue to carry it

Tired, trampled
The worn rug beneath your feet...
Used...

Comfortless Existence

This human skin that I've been given
It hurts and it itches, and it feels so foreign
Something inside is begging to be free
A desire to be more than what they've made of me
I am both exactly as I was created
And nothing at all that has been dictated

If I could just take it off for a day or two
Walk around in the body of someone new
Then maybe I would know what it means to feel right
Maybe I would understand why I cringe at the sight
Of this vessel the universe saw fit to bestow
And learn more about the being I dare not show

A Common Tale

A heart again breaks
In that isolated place
Surrounded by self-made illusion

A future now bleak
Resolve growing weak
Wading through this confusion

Alone here to wander
No love left to squander
Yearn for all that feels wrong

The past creeping in
A reminder of sin
Haunted by familiar song

Madness consumes
In guilt-painted rooms
Built by this tortured mind

A hand reaches out
Expecting the doubt
Common tale of ill-fated time

Road Blocks

Not one clear thought
Stuck
Shackled to the emptiness without a key
No hairpin, no tool that could be used to remove this weight
The pen stops
Nothing
Re-read, and read again
No word comes easily
Where is the inspiration I had yesterday?
The muse of my past has abandoned me
But what of the future?
Irrational are such hopes
And I'm out of Ink

Paper Wings

Another rainy day
The sky laden with thick, dark clouds
On a window sill she sits
Staring out over the dying garden beneath her
It's been months since she's tilled or planted,
watered or pruned
Months since she's even stood atop the soil
This dreary house has been her prison
Her only escape lies within this little corner
With its old-fashioned cushion
Covered in little blue flowers
And the loose wood plank beneath her feet
Where she hides her treasures...

She sits for hours
Thankful for the time he is away
Watching the world pass her by unknowingly
A bruise here, scratches there
Just enough time for these to heal
Before he lays a fresh set upon her skin
With a sigh, the kind that makes one weep with longing,
She removes the plank
And pulls out the small leather bag within
A couple of pens & pencils
Scissors, tape, scraps of paper, buttons, odds and ends
A purity ring, the diamond now lost to pay some
random debt
The only thing she has left to remember her mother by

She lays her scattered dreams around her
And sets to work on a pair of little wings
The finishing touch for her latest creation

The angel she'll hide behind her bed to protect her
when the darkness descends
When he comes for her

Silent as she cuts & shapes the paper
She imagines putting the flimsy things on herself
Taking a running start through the decaying back door
And soaring away from here, far away from here
Somewhere exotic and lovely
Where women dance and men romance
Where children spend the days playing in the surf
As their adoring parents take pictures from the shore
Where she will have a new name
A new family
A new life

But it will never be that simple
Alas these paper wings will never free her from this cage
She is a prisoner here
And her captor will return, time and again
If only to remind her of her fate

Diligent

A second string player on the sidelines
waiting for my turn to stand center stage
Always settling
Always second-guessing
Because it's what I do best
It's what I've always known
Not at the bottom
Yet not near the top
Left to waste away somewhere in the middle
The crippling truth that I've caused it all along
refuses to break the surface
And so the cycle continues again

The Uncertain Path

Cannot find the right words,
Or even the wrong words
Desperate to put pen to paper and let the ink wash away your sins
Fearing your greatest gift may be lost,
Lost in the chasm of your own self-defeat
And the deeper you search, the further it slips away

Despite these times where you strain to overcome,
Continually striving to sort the tangled mess of thoughts
To find the rhyme,
The reason for the chains that hold you down
You know it is nothing more than a feeble attempt to fly without wings

They cannot begin to understand the depth of this anguish
The pain it causes as it refuses to be released
Aching to shine once more, to be whole once more
Yet, without the inspiration you so desperately seek
You are simply an artist without a canvas, a shell without life

The Violence I Crave

The taste of this torture
so sweet and sharp on my tongue

Over and over again
you break me with savage dominance
With a hand around my throat
and a snake inside my body

It fills me with poison
as I beg for another injection
I am addicted to the deceit
to the pain you are so practiced at inflicting

The shame is nothing
I am content to live in these chains
these ties that bind me to your madness

Every bruise you lay upon my skin
Every scar that you made me deserve
Every drop of blood you extract
is another gift I crave to submit

Circle the Drain

You see it all

The despair
The confusion
The rage
The disillusion

You feel it seep inside
Eating
Festering
Poisoning

You take advantage
of each precious, momentary respite
so few and far between
Before fading back through
the veil of detachment
shrouding your weathered soul

You wait in tense apprehension
for that day when it will all come
crashing in
as it always has

Jaded Dreams of an Un-Mother

Handprints of all sizes left on a fractured heart
Those little reminders of all that was given
and all that was taken away
Tear open that constant wound, the one that never really heals
and bleed for another blameless soul destined to become a scar
No more
Though you yearn for a gift that should simply be yours to bear
as you watch the undeserving piss it away
You cry in solitude for the absence
the connections that were destroyed in the wake of lovers run aground
And the absence of a moniker that has never been uttered
You close yourself off from those opportunities to ever arise again
Board up your desire to dive in headfirst
to care too much
to abandon all sense in the name of a child's love
No one really understands
No one really has time for a selfish little girl who has sacrificed so much
Simply to be forgotten by those who weren't old enough to remember her name
No one really asks how you survive that kind of pain
The breaking of bonds built in chaotic existence
The curse of a woman whose hope is far too big to carry
Yet feels empty as the womb that never gave life

It Never Leaves

It never leaves
Not really
Always biting at the heels of its determined prey
Creeping so closely
The maddening scratch of its desires
The rancid smell of defeat on its tongue
It's toying with you
Letting you believe the space between is widening
Allowing you faint flickers of hope
Makes the feast quite delectable in the end
You tire of the battle for control
Growing immeasurably weak from the exertion
The mere thought of continuing to fight
Has you on the ropes
Ready to let the darkness consume
Swallow you up in its insatiable jaws
Your persistence only feeds its craving
Why not stop, rest awhile?
It must be gone
You pushed further than you ever thought possible
Further than you ever had before
All is quiet
All is still
As the warmth just ahead begins to wash over you
Ever so light upon your skin
Close your eyes and breathe deep
Take in this miniscule moment of victory
Remember every detail
Before that familiar feeling invades your bones
And that crushing weight crashes against your peace
You've always known
It never leaves

Suicidal

It's just so easy
A perfectly placed slice of the knife
Too many pills to drown out the noise
The deafening permanence of a gunshot

The ending, it comes swiftly
In utter juxtaposition with unyielding existence

I lost her, I lost him
I nearly lost both of them
I myself gave in to the noose
Stepped one foot across the veil from which we don't return

I was lucky
I had a hand that ripped me back
But once you have witnessed what lies beyond
You're never quite the same

You experience the mortal world in ways most cannot understand
And you begin to see the wood for the trees

It is a blessing, and it is a curse
And every so often you find yourself glancing into the darkness
As you ponder if staying
Is worth all of the breaking

An Evening With Death

"Come with me." The creature extends a deathly pale hand, the tips of each finger seemingly dipped in ink. "Let me show you what I see." I hesitate, but the intrigue is far too enticing, so I grasp it. Though I expected it to be icy, it is surprisingly warm. Before I can even blink, we are standing at the edge of a bed. The room is cozy, yet something about it feels hollow. A woman with a weathered face and silver hair lays beneath the covers - her eyes are closed, her breathing is shallow, and somehow I can hear the heartbeat in her chest waning. I glance around to find a display of somber faces, some with tears, some with sad smiles. I realize I am witnessing the moment when a soul leaves this plane of existence, and my breath catches.

The creature places its hand between my shoulder blades, invoking a strange sense of calm. "This is her time. This is her acceptance. She has lived a full life, and embraces her impermanence." All of a sudden, the heartbeat stops and I feel a presence beside me that wasn't there a moment ago. I look over to see her visage smiling down at her mortal vessel, no signs of anguish or anger in her soft eyes. She shifts her gaze to each face surrounding the bed and pauses on each one, likely committing them to her soul's memory. The silence is deafening until it breaks with the first sob, coming from the woman sitting at her side holding her now limp hand. The resemblance is uncanny - it's her daughter. My heart cracks at this sight, as if I can see myself in her, and feel her pain as if it is my own. The creature moves around me and holds the old woman by her bony wrists. They stare at each other, the only sound around us is the quiet cries from the loved ones she has left behind. And then the creature speaks. “What a magnificent blessing. I will cherish each one. You are ready now for the journey that must come.” The old woman nods as she slowly evaporates into nothingness.

“What did you do to her?” I whisper, eyes wide and body trembling.

“What I came to do. Does it still not make sense to you?” I shake my head, reeling from the complete lack of understanding. “She shared her life with me, as all beings must. I witness their entire mortal existence as a sign of trust. Then I hold their memories within me, a container of life for all eternity. No one is forgotten, no soul left unseen, and I send them on their journey to the worlds in-between.” I ponder on this as the scene around us fades and we stand in complete darkness. “Ask your question, I can sense the yearning. This rare glimpse of my fate is all about learning.”

I swallow the lump forming in my throat, for the answer to this question may unravel me. “What about those who...don't live a full life - whose existence is cut short, or even barely begins?” Without a word, the surrounding black fades into pure chaos. Red and blue lights flash, sirens blare, voices are shouting from every direction. At the center of it all, a horrifying scene of shattered glass and twisted metal, the scent of blood and gasoline permeating the air. A woman screams to my left, her agonizing cries piercing the air as a lifeless body is pulled from the wreckage. To my right, a child no more than ten watches his mortal form being zipped up into a black bag, never to feel the sunlight on his face or run carefree through the rain ever again. He looks over at me, eyes filled with incomprehension, and I am brought to my knees. The creature kneels before this innocent soul, taking his wrists and holding his gaze, just like the old woman. "Thank you for each memory," it finally says, its voice more caring and gentle than fits its appearance, "I shall always carry them with me. Now run along darling, your grandfather waits for thee." And the boy slowly dissipates as a wide smile spreads across his face.

"How can you be so calm?!" I shout, the pain and anger at a life left unlived coursing through my veins. "That boy had so much left undone, unseen, unexperienced! He was eviscerated! You're a monster!" My cries mingle with the mother who has just lost her child, and I am lost within the waves of unrelenting pain.

"I understand your suffering, and the desire to place blame. But I am not responsible for the way in which each soul passes, or the timeframe. My only assignment is to bear witness, to greet them as they arrive, and offer a sense of completion before they move on to await the next life." I wipe my eyes and regain my composure as I stand, still shaken, but growing steadier. Then I look up to see the creature's face, fully for the first time, and what is staring back at me nearly knocks me down again. It is my mother's face - gentle, loving, kind, and full of adoration. "You see, my child, I am merely a representation. Each soul experiences a very different version. A mother, like you, that is most common. Perhaps a lover, or a friend, whatever form the soul does summon. This visage presents an element of comfort - a reason to feel safe and cared for, so that their fear I can subvert. I do not know who is chosen, or why, or when, simply that I must be there for them."

The scene has once again faded into a void, and I am reeling from this experience. "So, I imagine you're here because it's my time? Why else would have shown me all of this?"

"You are not yet ready to pass through the veil, though you surely tried, but to no avail. Every so often I grace a soul with my perspective, I share my experience and my directive. You have been gifted a glimpse of the world beyond, and knowledge to possess as your life carries on. I will see you again one day, dear child. But I certainly hope it won't be for quite a while."

With that, everything goes black, and my eyes slowly open to the beeping of machines. I feel weak, and the lights are too bright.

"She's waking up!" Someone exclaims. A hand squeezes mine...funny, I hadn't felt it a moment ago. The room slowly comes into focus as I notice a tube in my throat and what feels like a needle in my arm. "Hey, take it slow." I recognize the voice, but my brain isn't processing it. I roll my head slightly to the side, and as I see the face floating there, the memories start to come crashing in fragmented images. The bathroom counter, my harrowing reflection in the mirror, the bottles of pills, the cold tile floor. My eyes widen as she looks down at me, a mix of sympathy and pity swirling within hers. "You're okay. You're gonna be okay." I can't speak - between the tube, the raw aching in my throat, and the sheer panic setting in, I am unable to ask any questions. As if reading my mind, she says, "I found you and called the paramedics. They pumped your stomach. A minute or two later, and..." she trails off. I muster as much strength as possible and squeeze her hand. She smiles, and in that moment I realize how lucky I am to be alive. As I process what I just experienced, I can't be sure it was real, but there is a part of me that believes it was, and I know I will never forget my evening with Death.

The Beauty of Love & Lust

Now we get to the fun parts - the passion, the intimacy, the moments that sparked my sexuality and ignited my deepest fantasies. I've always considered myself lucky in lust...not so much in love, that has been more of a battlefield. But I have learned many lessons from each relationship in which I have shared my heart, and many more from each lover who has shared my bed. I believe we need a less judgmental and more inquisitive perspective of the human sexual experience - it's not something that should invite shame, regret, or disgust. It is a beautiful, messy, transcendent part of all life. I understand, deeply & personally, how negative sexual encounters can affect our feelings surrounding it - I only hope to help redefine that in some small way. Not all my experiences were good, in fact, some of them were rather traumatic. Yet I would be lying to myself if I didn't admit that most of them brought me great pleasure, and a deeper love for my body in its most natural, vulnerable state.

Before

Dreaming was easier
before memories were made
in perfect little raindrops upon the path
Silence was easier
before words were spilled
like young lovers' blood upon the altar
Pretending was easier
before crossing the invisible
those intangible lines upon the divide
Desire was easier
before ecstasy lingered in waves
laced with absolution upon the bare
Breathing was easier
before sighs of life from such lovely lips
fell heavy upon my existence

Beloved

The moonlight cascades across her bare body
painting the fair flesh in a silvery glow

Hair splayed about the satin pillows beneath her sultry features
Intense eyes of ocean blue speak of all she'll never have to say
A sharp tongue glides across the surface of full, ripened lips
as her back arches in hungry anticipation

She wants only me
She craves only my touch
Every curve of her divine form is mine to devour
With just a look, she awakens the man I've yearned to be

I lightly run my fingertips along the surface of her skin
watching her quiver with desire
Moans of pleasure feeding the fire
A breath catches in her throat and I know I've found the spot

Slow & smooth
Hard & depraved
She wants it every way I can give it
And I give it all,
Just to taste her ecstasy
Just to watch her succumb

Instigator

She saw him
and she knew it to be true
yet, knew nothing at all
It was there
just hovering above the inevitable
waiting for its moment
Patient
Silent
Resolute
Snaking the idea of its true purpose
through every psyche
except the one that mattered most

No, she was left ignorant
Unmarked by the thought
of what more could be
She had to decide
She had to take the leap
or all would be for naught

A hint here
A little spark there
Something to keep her guessing
keep her thinking
keep her focused while throwing her off balance
And she loves it

No Stranger to Pain

Into a guarded heart he saunters
as it wonders what he ponders
While miles away she stands alone
a Princess of stone atop her throne

Fear of what she does not speak
"What do you seek?" she asks quite meek
A soul searching for its reflection
longs for perfection in this affection

This creature who presents a certain allure
Tragedies cure with a look so demure
Pleading with the fickle stars above
For a taste thereof his torturous love

Silent Assurance

Lay your head in my lap
As we wait in silence for the goodbye that always comes

Cradle my face in your hands
long enough for the warmth to remain well after I've
gone

Let me breathe you in deeply
that I might close my eyes and still have you beside me

Leave a parade of kisses upon my neck
like precious little secrets you whisper as I sleep alone

Embrace me in your strong arms
to keep me safe and guarded when I must steal away

Write deeply of this great love
words etched into the stars that blanket my lonely
shores

Worship at the altar of my existence
while you are made a wealthy king by my very touch

Give me willingly all that is mine
and I shall always return to give all that is yours

A Kingdom of Desire

Clawing
Biting
Bodies lie naked & exposed
Tender to the touch
But the poisonous tongue of pain
Excites, entices
Smothered anger & frustration
Manifest upon the wings of passion
A Queen
Relinquishes all control
A King
Relishes unyielding dominance
The Fool
A servant to both
Wickedly dancing
In this devil's playground
For the sake of a moment in heaven
Come, innocent sinner
Ignite these flames
Beg at her feet as she gives all to you
Rip away layers of insecurity
Starve such maddening fears
Purge the demons
Through her submissive flesh
surrender to your craving
and bask in its rapture
Your release shall be rewarded
With agonizing ecstasy

Formidable

The sweet taste of lips
upon flesh burdened with experience
Just a simple touch never felt
burns the surface of this façade with truth
An intricate web of words
built to capture a distinct prey
glittering in the first rays of a new dawn
attracts the attention of a far more formidable creature

Quiet Calm

This quiet calm
Defender against the noise
That held hostage my diminishing light
It crept in slowly,
Carried on the laughter
Of two travelers, whose paths almost never crossed
Too wary to just believe
Too jaded to hold out hope
Yet it never caved in, never faltered
Every irrational fear met with stark reason
Every reservation logically laid to rest
The further we walk this path together
The better for our darkest chapters we become
The better for each other we become

Raptor

Those eyes...
Those wickedly entrancing windows to the soul
Do you know what that gaze can do?

Do you see how they unnerve?
How they unravel?
With a raptor gaze that cuts through every wall,
every reservation,
every guard so carefully placed

You see all those little secret treasures
hidden deep within the darkest corners
from those that would dare turn a heart
to stone

You don't, do you?
Wielding such stunning weapons
with no thought of their deadly power
no care for the alluring authority they command

Just a broken soul
drowning in the wake of poisonous desires
holding the smallest breath of hope
for a rescue from your jaded kingdom

Just a Taste

The voice that gives no quarter
Thoughts that persist against better judgment
Nagging
Questioning
Confusing
Simply begging to be given an audience

An off-chance that tugs at the heart's resolve
It cannot be
But it will not dissipate
Presenting an allure of the unknown
The unrelenting pummel of the fascinating

What is it about the intrigue that tantalizes in such a way?
Why is it an ever-present distraction?
Will it ever cease?
Or is this just the accepted madness of a being sick with greed?

Alice & Her Hatter

Journey with me down the rabbit hole
where madness consumes all reason
A world built on relinquished control
far from the tale previously written
Dream intertwines with nightmare
wrong is so much more than right
Another unyielding beast to ensnare
A new battle to unwittingly fight
The queen of hearts plays with her toys
turning love to disgust & freedom to fear
Yet they stand in defiance, forever conjoined
Soon the path will be painfully clear
A past that can no longer be forgotten
the bond that can no longer be denied
Now that this candor has been spoken
Beyond insanity, these two souls collide

One

So what if I just let it happen?
What if I let you touch me, taste me, unravel me?
What if I only gave you the just once?
Would one simple touch be enough to quell the urge?

I think not
One would break the levies
One would topple this uneven kingdom
One would never be enough
Yet, what would be enough?
Would I find myself exactly where I started again?
Behind my mistakes & ahead of my heart
Would I wear you out like those that came before?
Those who could never be enough
I'm not so sure anymore...

As You Wish

Whisper your craving
in a sigh upon my neck

Beg for boundless pleasure
trailing lightly across my flesh

Confess away each sin
in kisses along my thighs

Reveal your truest self
As I rip away the disguise

Profess your promises
in treasures upon my lips

Release those binding chains
while digging fingers into my hips

Offer your imperfections
for the warmth of my embrace

Transmute this life of anguish
within the fires of my grace

Trade all of that longing
for the bliss of my seduction

Remind me I am yours
with not a single word spoken

Chapters

In the most unexpected of places
He was there
Where she had already been before
Where she had found something expected
Something she was searching for

It changed her
Destroyed her
Shaped her to fit a perfect mold
that had never really existed
It had been more
It had been less
then she had could have ever conceived

A truth
Buried deep beneath the intricate deceits of desire
A lesson
Meant to be learned in the most painful of ways

She had sworn never again
Yet, she was there

It all appeared no different
The same cracked walls painted a new hue
The same lost souls pining for connection
The same reeking scent of depravity & desperation

She sat at the bar
Keeping fair distance from the egos demanding a
chance
And the cynical burning their jealous stares into her
skin

This time around
Searching for nothing
Simply content to enjoy a drink or three
Comfortable in guarded silence

It wasn't arrogance
Keeping her at arm's length from the patrons
Nor jaded fear
More an experienced idea
That nothing in this place was ever truly
What it seemed

But when she saw him sitting there
Just a few stools down
Feverishly attacking paper with pen
A nearly empty glass of Bourbon at the helm
That idea faltered

She watched him briefly
Unable to keep her eyes from wandering
And she took a chance

She had the barkeep refill his drink
And simply waited
Not daring to steal another glance

It wasn't long before he sauntered over
Full glass in hand
Taking up post at the empty seat to her right

There was no exchange of words at first
They just sat together
And apart
In appreciation
In anticipation

In deep breaths of mutual understanding

"So you're a writer"
She finally began

"I'm an observer"
He replied smoothly
"A barstool prophet, if you will"

She smiled then
Knowing he was something indeed
Something unexpected
Something unlike anything

And so
Drink after drink
At a pub spilling over with sin & poetic dissonance
between the folds of brazen conversation
A new chapter finds its main characters

Devil with An Angel's Smile

They move their ripened lips
to the words that pour from the stage
Vows of pain and passion
and all they fear to truly feel

They move for you, these delectable delights
They sway to the charms you wear beneath your mask
Every eye on the star of the show
as the music flows fluidly around you

Masterful fingers stroke keys & strum chords
The rhythmic trance of the crowd feeds you
as you weave a spell of villainous intent

Bodies bared, supple flesh exposed
All are waiting for the feast
A fantastic nightmare so close
they can feel the blood pulsing in your veins
and they desire what they know they shouldn't

They beg for more
of which you are always obliged to provide
and they will return, time & again
for a small taste of what lies within your soul

Unsatisfied Craving

Let me tear away those layers
that shield you from the recurrence of pain
Beg of me
all which you fear to lose
Lay your scattered mind in the cradle of my hope
and wear my strength as a second skin

Do you dare it?
Would you risk the consequence?
Can the weight of uncertainty
hold back the flood of unsatisfied craving?

When reservations falter
When your soul pines for the release
that only I can offer
The scent of longing
wraps this moment
in a truth that haunts the darkest corners of my dreams

A truth that would condemn us
that would destroy us
that would set us both free

Subjugation

Claw your way to the fertile soil on which I stand
Kneel at my feet and beg for sweet release
Dig your fingers deep into my thighs
As you pray at the altar of this sexual awakening
Convincing my desire that you can earn this
subjugation
Show gratitude for the chains I bestow upon you
And I will feed your craving with unyielding pleasure
I will fill your cup to overflowing with sinful satisfaction
Your kingdom will be made great by my demands
The world will tremble before the power you command
Second only to the authority of my universal rule

Entice

The dreams unseen
The path less traveled
The constant evolution
I live for it, I crave the spice

The part of me hardest to please
is the constant ache for something new
Are you up to that challenge?
Can you surprise me over and over again?
Do you long to show me what I never knew existed?
Will you strive to experience everything with me?

You'd be the first
And the last
if you can simply promise a break from routine
Fill my cup with flavors I've never tasted
Paint my stories with colors I've never seen
Weave my future with words I've never read
Build my fortress with songs I've never heard

Do this, and I will bring your deepest fantasies to life

Collide

Stepping off the plane, I am surrounded by a sea of unfamiliar faces. Yet a feeling of comfort draws my attention to only one. There, a mere twenty feet away, I spot him and my heart skips. Everything around ceases to exist - all that matters is this moment and this man. For months, I have played every scenario out in my head, imagining every possibility, planning every detail carefully. Yet nothing I did could prepare me for this man. I stand there briefly. Then, silently begging for a bit of clarity, I make my way over to the radiating soul before me. I feel him before I even start moving again, his energy tugging me in the right direction.

Calm, cool, collected he stands; one hand in the pocket of well-worn jeans, the other holding a lit cigarette to his lips. Never mind the no-smoking sign above his head. Tousled brown hair and a five o'clock shadow speak of a man who has no care for others' critiques. Dark glasses hide his brilliant green eyes, but I can see through all of it - the subdued, yet ever-apparent 'fuck you' attitude, the reckless abandon for silly rules, the tortured genius lying beneath a common ideal. The type of man who sees deeper into your soul than you knew existed, pulling out even the most hidden specks of madness you hold in the darkest of places and putting them on display.

He puts out his cigarette and smiles knowingly. Two feet away I stop and close my eyes, breathing him in. A second later, I am tightly wrapped in his embrace, a feeling of peace surrounds and invades my entire being, a feeling only his spark could ignite. We hold each other in perfect bliss forever, as time no longer matters, followed by a deep kiss stained with craving, barely scratching the first few layers of satisfaction. As we pull away, the hustle of the world around us fades in, but we are no more aware of these simple distractions than they are of us. I take a moment to catch my breath.

"Are you ready?" he asks.

"For anything..." is my reply. This is our only exchange of words.

Making our way out of the airport towards his car, I hold him close as he firmly grips my hand and leads the way. I'm almost waiting for the beauty to fade out into that heartbreaking haze when you realize it was all just a dream. A perfect gentleman, he holds my door open and closes it as I settle into my seat. As the engine starts, the radio comes alive and a familiar sound escapes the speakers, permeating throughout the space between us... *'I'll keep you in my arms for sure...'* That knowing smile spreads across his lips as he backs out of the parking space, and again I am comfortably lost. Driving down the highway, all is silent except for our song, which is on repeat, as expected. So many words push to break free from their chains, but I dare not speak, only take it in and let it be.

As if reading my mind, as per usual, he looks over at me with those soulful pools of swirling jade and asks, "Speechless?"

"Aye, a thousand words, but none to speak."

“That's ok beautiful, no words need be said...secret languages,” to which he gives a little wink, taking my hand into his. A flow of undulating emotion through each of us now joined with the simplest gesture.

We reach our destination, a small coffee shop secluded from the bustle of the sheep and their herders, and find a quiet corner outside. The waitress makes her way over as he lights my cigarette, ever the gentleman.

“Dark Roast, Irish cream.”

He doesn't even wait for her to ask, but she doesn't miss a beat, “And for you miss?”

“French Roast, dash of cream and sugar. And a couple buttered croissants, please.” She heads off with our order, and we sit in comfortable silence for a minute or two.

“Why so quiet?” he asks, finally removing his sunglasses. I can see all the beauty & pain he locks away from the world in those magnificent eyes, and my own secrets beg to be entwined with his.

“Just taking it all in. The very definition of ethereal...and I'm sitting here in the eye of the storm.”

“Aye, almost a dream, but unlike any dream I could have ever hoped to come true.”

The waitress descends upon us, drinks and pastries in hand. She places them on the table and asks if we need anything.

"Nothing at all,' I think, *'it's perfect.'* I thank her, shaking my head. Away she walks; we finally find ourselves alone.

The next few hours breeze by; insightful ramblings of everything and nothing over multiple cups of coffee, the simple conversation of two souls whose mutual understanding surpasses that which few others can even comprehend. As the sun begins to set, we decide it's time to make our way elsewhere and pay the bill.

Again we are in the car, almost floating on the melodies of our song, *'the places you're taking me to'.* A short time later, we arrive at his condo - down a narrow path from the parking lot, spring erupting in the flower bushes and trees that line the brick path, second door on the left. He opens it and lets me step inside first. There's a perfect amount of light from the big window at the back of the room; to the left, a kitchen and small dining area. Straight away, he leads me to his bedroom. There's nothing sexier than a man who wastes no time in attaining what he wants.

He looks right into my soul, and asks "Are you ready, my love?" I have no words to share, only feelings. I grab his head, fingers entangled in his hair, and pull his lips to mine, taking every second and locking them inside of me. He slowly unbuttons and removes my shirt, kissing every inch of my bare skin as he does, pausing briefly to admire the exquisite pink flesh of my nipples with his experienced tongue. I'm wrapped in ecstasy as he lays me down to slowly free my body from the strangling threads, tracing his fingers lightly along the outsides of my legs as he goes, and the force of his desire breaks free when he hungrily works his mouth back up between my quivering thighs. He aims to please, and as the first wave of my own desire crashes against his shores, I respond to his unequivocal skill in loud, unbridled moans of pleasure. For the rest of this enchanted evening, the world outside ceases to exist; we become so entangled that there is no telling where one starts and the other begins, suspended in pure bliss after a ravenous feeding upon our most sacred fantasies. As the sun rises, I lay in his arms, singing him to sleep, *'the hallways I wouldn't mind crawling through...'* We drift into dreams, allowing ourselves the rare opportunity of freedom from obligation, from reality. The beauty of this union surrounds me in my sleep, infiltrates my very being and puts my soul to rest. I am lost in this perfect imperfection.

As It Should Be

As a fog on the wind
the density of your adoration
lies sweetly upon my skin

Encase my passion
within the strength of your faith

Ignite my fantasies
within the subtlety of your yearning

Wear my happiness
as you would your favorite suit

I would dare traverse
the miles that divide
and breathe new life into your world
For the simple pleasure
of claiming this forever

Let me crawl around
inside your every thought
and drown in your waves of devotion

Seduce my mind
Intoxicate my senses
Arouse my soul

I will create the reality
we both deserve
from dreams now intertwined

Ambivalent Fascination

His mask portrays a man of unmarred confidence
that narrowly borders well-earned arrogance
Less keen eyes focus on the crafted performance
and miss the wicked scars beneath his dissidence

They know not of the inspiration he so craves
or the past he buries in a myriad of graves
Pining for his attention as would hopeless slaves
begging for a taste of madness, these incessant knaves

There is a beauty in his fractured sense of reality
Such an enigma wrapped in the deadly grip of duality
His intoxicating charm conveys the deepest sexuality
finding themselves lost within the layers of his
depravity

He works tirelessly to drown out the nagging pain
this shattered heart his life's ever-present bane
Weaving an intricate design of love he cannot attain
to cover the trauma that has built his magnificent
domain

All I Have to Give

This madness
This longing
This crippling desire
This anticipation
This conviction
This consuming fire
This freedom
This prison
This unyielding thirst
This fantasy
This possession
This soul immersed
This adoration
This aching
This pleading whisper
This past
This present
This boundless future

Driftwood

Lay me down on a cloud of sorrow
While I embrace the pain swimming in your eyes
Give me a reason to wake on the morrow
And just for you I'll blur these lines

Tempt my will with your imperfections
Whisper the words I dare not say
Break through the wall mortared with excuses
And the fears that keep this hunger at bay

Across the raging waters you stand
On the banks of a world I yearn to explore
Yet firmly planted I'll remain in this land
Until the unwavering vessel carries you to my shore

Not Quite Needy

I'll never ask much of you
I'll never expect more than I can give
I'll always give more...

Read to me
Play me songs that remind you of me
Talk with me
Listen
Hold me whenever you can spare a moment
Keep honesty in your pocket
And faithfulness on your sleeve
Try new things and see the world with me
Kiss me
Kiss me more
Adore me endlessly
Inspire me
Let me be myself always
And love me for all it entails
Share your dreams,
your desires and your fears with me
Take my breath away
with a look
or a word every day
Cherish me
Treat me as your equal
Find beauty in the mundane with me
Tell me of all you find breathtaking
Daydream with me
Cradle my heart carefully
Never stop being the man you are now...

I know what I deserve
I know my worth

I see the same in you
I'll be the same for you
Always...

Forty Years & Counting

A pair of lovers stroll leisurely among vibrant spring blooms
Eyes that have seen the darkest of times gaze fondly into the well-known soul of another
Weathered hands, worked hard for far too many years, hold each other with a firm tenderness

The comfort and ease of such a simple task subtly conveys an unbreakable bond
forged through the sharing of every emotion along our great spectrum
and the will to fight for that which every being deserves

A different time
A different way of life
A foundation & dedication that were built to last

They stop for a few moments of rest and he helps her to a bench,
making sure she is comfortable before taking the seat beside her
They soak in the delightful scene surrounding
Still hand in hand,
Content within a serene silence

Dark hair has given way to gray
The wear on their faces tells a lifetime of stories
Of triumph & sadness
Of love & loss
Of worry & relief
He watches her now, with a look upon his face as if he's seeing her for the first time,

while she takes notice of a young couple across the path,
locked in a warm embrace

She smiles softly,
perhaps reminiscing back to their first journey through this park
or that enchanting evening when he asked her to be his wife
Right on this very spot
He can see her thoughts; hear the whispers of her heart
And he steals a sweet kiss as she turns to face him,
catching her by surprise
The young couple passes then,
And the woman smiles at this intimate exchange
between lifelong lovers

Heartbreak - Life's Greatest Teacher

Ah, the suffering that comes in the wake of our strongest, most complicated emotion. Love has shattered me on several occasions. It has lifted me from the depths of despair and shoved me right back down into the pits of hell; it has both created a sense of self-worth and destroyed every bit of self-worth I have ever had; it has shaped me, rearranged me, put me on a pedestal far too high, and failed every expectation I have forced upon it. These next pages are filled with the jagged pieces of a heart that has been glued back together over and over again through awareness, platonic relationships, and learning every lesson love's painful sting has taught me. While I wish some of those tests had not been part of the assignment, I am trying to give myself more grace, and accept the fact that I cannot change what was, only move forward into what will be with a deeper sense of self and better understanding of what love truly should be.

And So It Goes

Always a whirlwind
Beginnings with so much potential
Heaps of promises to compromise
Miles of road ahead to embrace the balance
Years of lessons from which to draw experience
Then, as it goes...

The experience gives way to routine
The balance grow ever so tiresome
The compromise all too easily forgotten

Passion & lust
The bait that lured you in
Exquisite, sobering against a darkened past
Mesmerizing
Intoxicating
Sublime hunger dripping with a hidden poison
Aimed at a soul full of faith

Where once affection stood
Now only numbness sits
Where once love held the pen
Now only habit writes the story
Where once dreams were shared
Now only sleep fills the silence

The cycle never changes

And so it goes...

Artist

I knew a man once
A beautifully tragic, broken man
with eyes that even the stars would envy
and a smile that illuminated the night sky
His dominating presence rearranged my universe from the first shy glance
Little wonders filled the darkness
with glowing embers of hope & passion

Watching him strum that old guitar,
strong hands making love to each chord,
I wanted nothing more than to be the muse through which he could shed his pain
I would have given anything
I gave everything

Lying awake in the black stillness of this dream,
feeling the warmth of his body radiating next to mine,
I would invent new ways to grant him pieces of my soul
Bartering my needs for another taste of his desire

This cunning artist who painted such an inspiring illusion of love
I fell in love with that illusion
I was misled, I was deceived
by an overwhelming sadness shrouded beneath each brush stroke
and I learned that lesson too late

"Never fall for an artist" my mother had said
"You'll never live up to the true object of his affection – himself"
But I didn't listen

I fell for the fantasy
for the unattainable vision of perfection that was never truly present

Beneath the breathtaking sculpture of flesh & blood,
that man did not exist
Such a cruel & painful reality
One I was not prepared to face, even as I knew it to be true
Even as he lied, used, cheated,
and broke every promise that fell from his delectable lips
Even when I saw him kiss her with those lips I stayed,
some part of me believing my love would eventually be enough
But it never was

Now, even as those memories have long since been laid to rest
their ghosts return to haunt me from time to time
Perhaps to remind me of my mistakes
so that I never fall prey to such false beauty again
or maybe to simply show me how much love I can give
Unconditionally
Selflessly
even when it destroys me

Whatever the reason,
I thank them for reminding me that I am human

I knew a man once
A lost and exquisitely tortured man
I could not save him,
but in some strange twist of fate,
he ended up saving me

Playing With Boys

Sneaking looks at her across the table
Then flashing your smile at the one you claim to love
Just a game for you
Like a cat with a string, two dangling toys there to play with
Two fragile hearts
Two willing souls
Two foolish girls
One who is all that you'll ever need
and one who needs all you'll never give

Strong and confident in her coveted place at your side
She stands against the storm of the other's interference
She is a hero, a savior, she needs to feel needed
And her pride refuses to give you up that easily
You belong to her and her alone

While there she lingers, the ghost from your past
Salivating at the chance she never had with you
She truly believes herself entitled
Yet she has no idea the damage her arrogance will cause
Nor the steep price tag that comes in the aftermath

Back and forth you lie with each, lie to each
Begging her forgiveness for something you said you hadn't done
Calling her crazy for thinking you could ever betray her
Even as she watched you betray her
You love the one and not the other
You want the other and not the one
It must be exhausting to keep up such a delicate charade
And yet, you play your roles effortlessly

"I will only break your heart"
She should have listened, should have taken heed
Should have seen the trail of bloody pieces from those who came before
But that's what the delusions of love do
Blind us, deafen us, dull our senses, and deny our intuitions
Just long enough to tear us to shreds

Alas, she will leave
She will finally see you for what you really are, who you really are
It will be the hardest thing she will ever do
And she will question herself for days, weeks, months, maybe even years to come
But when all is said and done
She will be the better for it, for every single minute of it
And she will create a life that you could never imagine

Cheater

What-if's and would-have's
bury themselves deep within the shadows of sub-consciousness
Pure desire for what should have been
A yearning to satisfy that which must not be obliged

The light flutters in a space that belongs to another
yet an undeniable truth lies white-hot across Pandora's box

Such a sin to open the floodgate
A stunning tragedy to behold
Even as the words trickle through cracks
in the barrier between two momentary dreams in time

Nothing will change the course of what was
and the will to act has long since passed

Two souls reconnected across the miles
to confess a regret they unknowingly shared
A mistake that can never be unmade
So here is written the romance left un-allowed to flourish
the gut-wrenching question of "why now?"
can never rearrange what is

Boxing Match

Back and forth, the fight ensues
Consumes
Throwing punches in the dark
Overthinking
Overwhelmed
Underestimating the anticipated
Section off the truth
Behind thick walls
Only to allow seepage through the cracks
Speak of nothing
While alluding to something
The urge to control the uncontrollable
creates a myriad of denials
There is contentment
There is comfort
Yet, there is also strain and unrest
Selfish needs that cannot be met
A routine that belongs without belonging
Knowing without understanding
Unfair to feign acceptance on either side
When there surely isn't
Why must truth be so complex?

Disparagement

Blame her for the pain you feel
They all are at fault for a heart that lies in pieces
She didn't love me enough
She smothered me with her love
She wanted more than I could give
She couldn't give me more
She refused to stick around
when shit began to fall out of place
She wasn't the strength I needed
when her support was all I had

Never turn the spotlight on yourself
Never see the mistakes that keep you broken
Never make the changes that would save your soul
from all the darkness you've created

You...
You are the common denominator
in all those relationships you believe failed you
You are the guard
the keeper of your past
the mess that's left behind
You are the reason
she could no longer stand your presence
and the drowning misery
she could no longer struggle against

This is your choice, these are your demons
The longer you hold accountable
the countless lovers whom you've invited
The longer you will find yourself
treading water against a current
of your own jaded sins

Bridge Burning

"I'm sorry" he uses for his lead in
As if those words mean shit
As if you can just turn us back 'round and reset the hourglass
Those are the words of a coward in a costume

"You must know you are still in my dreams" he throws at me
As if I asked to be there at all
As if you somehow occupy any space in mine anymore
Those are the dreams of a boy in denial

"I was scared, I don't know what to do" he presents as his excuses
As if that has anything to do with me
As if you really believed I didn't want to hear the truth
Those are the lies of a child caught red-handed

"Please talk to me" he pleads in desperation
As if that will ever change the decision I've made
As if you'd even want to hear my reply
That is the last failed attempt at a bond now broken

Untitled 3

Tick, Tick, Tick
The madness of a second hand
All you want to do is smash that damn clock
Tick
But you can't
It was his clock
The only tangible reminder you have of his chapter in your book
Tick
Nothing drowns it out
Tick
Not even the waves crashing against the shore of your skull
The memories
The questions without answers
Tick, Tick
It's been months now
Tick
You can still smell him in the sheets you've washed a hundred times
Tick, Tick
The rhythm of his deep breaths has vanished
Replaced with the insanity of that damn clock
Tick
Torturing yourself just to hold onto a piece of this phantom
This ghost that turned away from all you had to offer
Tick, Tick, Tick
Never enough
Tick
~~Where the fuck is that hammer?!~~

Junkie

How dare you expect me to be
another thing on your list of need

Want
Desire
Crave
Treasure
But never need

Need is reminiscent of "can't live without"
Possessive
Controlling
Jealous
That will simply not do

I can't be your lover

You can't be my friend
Wrong time
Wrong place
Wrong circumstance

This is what has become of our history
Will you ever be able to look upon me
without the pain of what almost was?
Will I ever be able to trust you again
after you turned away from my honesty?

I know now
Painful as denying the ache would have been
I never should have allowed our lips to touch
I should have known then
how that one mistake would destroy us

Lovers Quarrel

A quiet sob gives way to screams
the questions have finally forced to the surface

"Why have you done this?"
"Do you believe I deserved it?"
"Did you really think I wouldn't find out?!"

A growing rage emerges
breaking through the barrier at your unending deceit

"Was she worth it?"
"Did you even stop to think of me?"
"Don't you understand the damage you've done?!"

A complete loss of control
pain now unleashing its ugly self to destroy its creator

"Where did I go so wrong?"
"Can you even begin to imagine this aching?"
"How can you sit before me with such an innocent face?!"

A deadly and irreversible mistake
the red of this fury now stains our memory with your secret betrayal

"Are you even listening?"
"Why are you just lying there?"
"Won't you please say something?!"

A moment of clarity
now seeing the bloody picture as it lies before me
"What have I done?!"

Something Like Closure

The night is dark, inky black without a star in sight to
comfort me

The air stale and warm, my throat burns with every drag
from my cancer, yet I continue to smoke, fighting the
true disease that eats at me

I am waiting...for what, I'm not sure...
An explanation?
An apology?
A declaration of remorse?
Anything...

As I drift back among the memories
I am faced with the reality I had, for so long, chosen to
ignore

So much time wasted drowning myself in your empty
words and forgotten promises

And now, the truth in your lies has been laid before me
and the blood from the battle that could not be won
stains this path I walk

I have descended from your high, landing hard on this
cold plane of existence

A picture perfect Love...but pictures can be deceiving,
and the canvas you painted to lure me is fading, wearing
so quickly with time passed

Blinded by feelings and underestimating the true nature
of the beast

A brilliant disguise, the soul I fell in love with has become lost behind his mask, forever catering to the fear that will keep him undiscovered, guarded and alone

I shed one last tear for that man, and leave the battlefield behind...

Long Dead Lovers

The first,
with eyes that still haunt your dreams
and that devilish grin
Left you breathless & weak
yet never even scratched the surface

The second,
with all the dreams of a child
and a decisiveness to match
Gave you passion & excitement
yet left out the reality

The third,
with promise on the tongue
and deceit within the heart
Lured you under entrancing spell
yet fell victim to fear of need

The fourth,
with such strong hands
and the tortured soul hidden well
Created a perfect little fantasy
yet drowned in a jaded past

The fifth,
with an artists' depth
and addiction to self
Brought you back full-circle
yet the lesson was finally learned

Social Commentary & Criticisms

As a Journalism Major, one of the things I have always been passionate about is current & historical economic, social, and political affairs. I tend to pull some of my best inspiration from things that are happening in the world around me, and in recent years I have had a lot to pull from. Fair warning, I don't care what way you lean politically, I do not prescribe to the system and will not be catering to either side in the following pages. I support humanity, equality, awareness, community, and balance between the masculine & feminine. In these pieces I call out those in power for their gluttony and shed light on the unyielding difficulties of simply existing as a woman in this world.

The P.I.C.

Awkwardly placed
upon the face of an empty promise
these infractions of
a well-calculated reality

Manipulated by forces unseen
bend this way, and that
as you slowly splinter
Just as they had hoped
Pieces of a soul, slivers of hope
that they've asked you to barter
The exchange isn't fair
The truth is unrecognizable

No masters of craft
nor pride are to be found
when the wielders of power
demand, yet don't deliver
on this fabricated creation
this freedom that doesn't truly exist
Or does it? we whisper

Like a woman in denial
about the abusive lover
She needs him
She loves him
He'll make it right, he'll do better
He swore he would

They feed you lies
to make you fat & lazy
they declare 'Change!'
But they don't really want it

This system
it wears well on them
like an Armani tailored suit
And you admire it
you aspire to it
For what?
For silly pieces of paper
and a whisper of peace?

Begging at their table
as would a dog for scraps
This is not
the means of survival
This is the controlled environment
of used car salesmen
and thieves of the masses

Detachment

In my land, suns do not rise
Moons do not glow
Barbed wire entwines the flowers
Their petals torn
Their roots shallow

In my land, vision is lost
Words lack inspiration
Stories weighed down by torment
truth strangled by fear of rejection

Everyone reads to feel, to escape
Yet there are no feelings
There is no escape

I am not sad, nor am I happy
Simply lost
Alone in the middle of a room filled with bodies
wearing familiar yet unknown faces

I don't need companionship
I don't want loneliness

In my land nothing is to be believed
Surrounded by falsity and unearned arrogance
Even when hidden, guarded
I am still sought out and shattered

You say I am dramatic
looking only for a reason to complain
but in my land
I am marked by the sorrow that swallows me

Optimistic Fool

I awaken to find myself missing
the bittersweet reality of my dreams
The comfort of them calls to me
every second I'm away

Yearning to escape the surrounding
Even my worst dreams seem somehow
better than this place
This world I walk
Rich in its ignorance, its greed
Its betrayal & selfishness
Disconnection through technological connection
Now aren't I a hypocrite

Basic instinct means nothing to these creatures
It is no longer simply Live, but
"How Perfectly I Live"
"How Untarnished I Live"
"How Others Perceive How I Live"

The means by which we meet our goals
is the expense of morality
of balance
Destroying all that we see to prolong our own suffering
Live forever
Horde it all
crush whomever or whatever stands in the way

Feeding off the divine life force
the very soil on which we stand
Until we get the satisfaction we so crave
then move on to the next

I crawl beneath my blankets
hoping tomorrow will see a different view
But knowing that
is no more than an exercise in futility

To Be a Girl

Such fickle disposition
from one swing to the next

Unprovoked jealousy
Unchecked insecurity
Piles of denials and delusions

Even the best of us
harbor moments of stark weakness
against the canvas we paint
for all the world to see

Demand your equality
while secretly stowing away hopes for a fairytale fallacy
Assert your dominance
of nothing more than waving your sexuality like a flag of empty conquest
Shout "Sisterhood!" from your tallest tower
as below mental warfare rages against the set of tits you view as competition

Oh, but to have been born with a cock!
Throw a few punches
then share an easy laugh over a simple beer
Declare frustration outright
without the mess of guessing games
To be forthright in your meaning
In your words and in your thoughts

Oh, what a liberation that would be...

Calculated Madness

Constant complication contrives
the calloused hands of communication

Cramped, cornered, constricted creatures
left craving for complete connection
In this culture of divisive dedication

Clarity creased by careless emotional clutter
Another classic case of complacency
claims this creation
Countless cackles echo of these corrugated crimes
As the cries of confession & candor seep through cracks
in this crumbling canyon

Those cliffs upon which contempt
corroded all capacity for human correlation
As consumerism creates a clouded perception

Clinging like a cancer to a candy-coated hierarchy
of crisp versus crinkled collars
Comply as would a criminal,
condemned by its own corruption,
to this crippled character of caution and conformity
And concede to this cloyed continuance
you call Life

Intangible

Seconds
Days
Years
Here, fit into this pretty little idea of ultimate finality
Oh, you thought you were on your time?
How silly of you
We've loaned you our time
We've given you only the time we think you need
And we've created a time frame for you to work within
Aren't we thoughtful?
The moment you arrive here,
We provide you with boundaries
We give you a picture of who you ought to be
And we expect you to follow that path
You will be condemned for daring to stray
You will be looked down upon for using our time
to serve your own ends
You will be rebranded as an outcast
And we will force down your throat
the proposition that this lifetime you dare speak of
is meant to be survived in conformity

See that clock there?
It's ticking away the moments we've allowed you
So use it wisely
Because this notion of immortality beyond the
constraints of time
doesn't agree with our plans
Hurry it up, little lamb
Fall in line with the rest
Doesn't it feel nice to relinquish all control and
accountability?

Misconception

Pretty little white dress of lace and frills
worn with a painted, angelic face
to convey your purity

Inaudibly narrating the picture
of ultimate submission

Lavish taste to mask the imbalanced bargain
As a guilty shadow waits
beneath the convenience of Faith
Binding the future
with shackles of domesticated obedience

A piece of flimsy paper
now dictates your every move
And your ancestors weep while
An impenetrable promise
now marks the beginning of your end

Those dreams you had colored
as a life so feverishly hoped for
are washed away
among the waves of expectancy

Place your belief
in this perfect deceit
only to be counted as a prized possession

Profess your misguided ideals
and seal this common fate
with a holy kiss

Empathy & Regret

Mourn not the soul
that wallows within the depths
of its own pity

Sing not the praises
of a man who guards himself
from the risk of chance

Share not in the misery
of a heart which refuses
the necessary change

Walk not the path
of a traveler who trembles in fear
to see its end

Dream not for the lover
who has no desire to gaze up
Eyes filled with brilliant stars

Write not the story
that drowns out faith for the sake
of explanation

Waste not a moment
on those who cannot see beauty
wrapped in the folds of anguish

Expect not from another
that which you yourself are unwilling
to give

Deadly Seduction

She sits there laughing at me with those deep emerald eyes, mocking me with those sultry lips drenched in crimson silk. Every flaw, every imperfection lies under her microscope; naked and exposed in the middle of a crowded room. I am invisible in my dark little corner, yet her judgments burn a deep hole inside my desire to touch her.

Her laugh rings out over the bustle of the bar, light and breathy. Some silly boy in uniform follows her like a lost puppy, noticeably uncomfortable and awkward; sweat beading on his forehead at the thought of having this goddess to himself. She entertains his advances, but only for the sport of it, she will not be his bedmate tonight, or any other night. She leads him to the dance floor as a haunting melody pours from the speakers. A simple white dress clings to her body, hugging her curves and showcasing her long legs, every secret laid bare.

As she moves and sways through the crowd, the men stare with a deep longing and the women glare with a deep loathing. She dances for me, this devil disguised as an angel, tossing her fiery mane. The boy becomes restless and impatient as she tires of his flaccid game. He sets his sights on a girl who will give him the ego boost he so craves, a girl he can manipulate, and again I am alone with her.

The blood in my veins boils from the radiant heat crawling along her milky skin. I am intoxicated by a flowery scent that permeates the air in the chasm that lies between us. Every inch of her is a weapon, sexual warfare designed to dull the mind and sharpen only the simplest of senses. She is a master of her craft, toying with a long string of hearts and awakening emotions once dormant. But tonight, she will become the toy. She will feel the searing pain of unbridled lust.

We will linger here until only a few remain, those who call this dingy hole home. She has saved herself for me this night, even if she does not yet know. In the dark, I will follow her. In the night, I will take her. I will show her a man in control, one who cannot be led to his demise by her siren call. She will beg for mercy, cry for release, and she will receive neither.

So, go ahead Temptress, walk past me as if I don't exist, as if you don't know my face. Overlook the man in the shadows who has long since pined for you in flowers and gifts and letters of love, who has given you every opportunity to declare the undying love you so easily deny. You will realize that you asked me for this, one way or another. Tonight, you will finally be mine, never again to lie in the arms of another victim before you tear his will to shreds.

Fucked

This...

This is not how we are meant to live
Fed scraps from a table
littered with the discord of their sins
Given little shreds
to keep the aching in our bellies barely at bay

We carry the weight of their wants
on our breaking backs
so they may taste the fruits of our labor

No room left to dream
No air left to breathe

We are bred to believe
that life is survived by their standards
that our daily struggle to maintain
is exactly what we deserve
We are bred to be their whores
the oldest profession indeed

They bend us over
shove our face down
in 1200 thread count Egyptian Cotton sheets
and plow us
without even the courtesy of lube
to make the raping a bit more bearable

And when they're finished?
They carelessly toss us to the side
a gaping hole of uselessness
they've no more need of

This...

This is the great lie
we've allowed them to dangle over our naive heads
You are free,
free to spend your life serving their means
and the best you can do
is smile through every bloody beating

Obedience Be Thy Name

Be soft
Be sweet
Clasp your hands and cross your legs
lest you tempt the scoundrels who cannot control themselves
Because that, of course, is your fault

Little ladies don't push back
Push away
Push buttons
They sit still
Stay silent unless spoken to
And always have a kind word ready to share

They wear a smile for every stranger
And a low-cut top for every set of lustful eyes
Yet always cover their bodies in shame
so as not to threaten the status quo

Ask politely and never decline
Give all of yourself, require nothing in return
Be gentle
Be helpful
Be grateful for the scrap heap you are gifted
Be everything that everyone expects, and nothing that they fear

Bury your rage deep in your bones
For that belongs to the boys

Fight your desires like a good girl
Extinguish the consuming fires that burn beneath your flesh
Fit the mold you are given
Or be cast as a deadly villain

Do not ask questions
Do not know more than your place in this world allows
Do not stand firm in your beliefs
Yet defend blindly the monsters who would devour you
Defile you, corrupt your light
Because they don't know any better
But you do

Survive in conformity
Thrive in heavy chains
Strive to be better, yet never contrive for more
This is what it means to be a woman

Gilded Purgatory

Stagnant
Stuck
Strangled
Cravings gone unsatisfied
It's this place
This disaster of distaste
Lacking sustenance, substance
Devoid of any real culture
Rich only in its arrogance and self-loathing
A history rooted deeply in deceit
How many masks can one wear?
Step right up,
Test your limits here!
Where being simply two-faced is for amateurs
Decade upon decade of failed dreams
Lying in heaps on every corner
Like garbage so easily discarded
Streets littered with decaying starlets & veteran hippies
Begging for I Owe You's
Greed separates the men from the boys
This is where Hollywood comes to die

Divinity Awakens

Beneath the guilt
The rotted tree of supposed Sin
The lies that have been sown in the soil atop her slumber
She stirs

For millennia
They have rewritten the Awakening
Shaped and shifted the blame
to suit their selfish, gluttonous desires
They have stolen the Divinity
And poisoned its roots
For the sake of their inadequacies

Her eyelids flutter
Her spirit breathes
Her Hands of Plenty dig through decaying dirt
Reaching for the sacred seeds of her womb
Her power rekindles in the darkness
As she ignites the truth in those who have always been listening

This crumbling structure of deceit
Built for those who walk blindly
Must be torn down
Destroyed
Decimated
To make way for a new beginning
A spiritual reckoning

"Wake up, my children..." she whispers,
"The time has come. The light awaits."

Will you heed her warning?
Will you welcome her bounty of balance?
Or will you fall to the might of her devoted,
Washed away in the flood of their enlightenment?

Choose wisely...

Shadow Work

One of the most important parts of any healing journey is the Shadow Work. Sadly, that's also a part that is often overlooked or simply avoided. I get it - taking a deep look at yourself and honestly being accountable for your own bullshit is not only hard work, it's immensely painful. You have to be willing to look your demons square in the eye, to accept that you have made mistakes due to a lack of awareness, to admit that you have hurt others in ways you may never have intended, and to understand that no one else is responsible for your reactions. Shadow Work reveals your truest self and forces you to integrate those unconscious aspects of your personality into the self you show the world - it's the only path to balance, emotional health, and psychological well-being. These pages are focused on my process through this painstaking work, and the pieces of myself that I've found along the way.

Pressure

The creaks & groans of a settling house
Straining its skeletal structure
causing hairline fractures in the bones upon
which it rests
Walls once so bright
Once so full of vivid life
have begun to fade at a startling rate
Chipping paint alludes to more wear
than the dweller would ever admit
Carpets worn with trample
Furniture stained with mistakes
Hundreds of smiles
from thousands of memories
crowd each room with framed stillness
Reminders of the indifference of time
It feels a prison
this once striking, yet humble abode
Like a small closet or cupboard
you've accidentally locked yourself inside
No use crying out
or pining for rescue
This is your vessel
And you are the only soul present

More Than Restless

Standing in the eye of this storm
raging within a complex mind
The fear of all that cannot be changed
breaks the heart of this lonely soul

Cannot be tamed
Cannot be caged
Cannot live this routine life
Begging for nothing more than a new & exciting view
Yet receiving only more of the same

Effort is given,
though it is not enough
Does that speak of selfish need?
Or unfulfilled promise?

No longer certain of the hope that once held the cards

Alibi

Desperately grasping for a reason
That wasn't me!
I wasn't there!

Excuse after well-worn excuse
plays off your tongue
like a politicians practiced speech

You know what you said, what you did
But you cannot accept those terms
Lying more to yourself than anyone else

It's a powerful addiction
this merciless self-doubt
this ragingly precarious nature

You wear the blood of these crimes
on your shaking hands
and you cannot deny the glaring evidence

This is the truth you refuse to acknowledge
These are your lessons
Commit them to memory

Or your soul will drown in darkness
your vessel will become hollow
and you'll only have yourself to blame

Faith Misplaced

Under the amused gaze
of eyes filled with misunderstanding
Shoulder the tragic burden
of a paragon weighed down with longing

Along the roiling surface
of an ocean without mercy
Burn beneath the blinding judgments
of so many souls unworthy

Between the blurred perceptions
of complex opinion & plain truth
Wear the thousand different masks
of a false dream painted aloof

Over the crimson-stained battlefield
of desire versus obligation
Detach yourself from the violent madness
of an unbeatable compulsion

Sometimes We Fail

It's been months
Can't bring myself to delete your number
Pictures of you found in unexpected places
Your laughter on the wind
Little reminders of your absence
Fill my quietest moments with regret
If I had only been better
Maybe I could've seen how far you'd gotten
How alone you'd grown
How deeply hurt you'd been
More attentive, more understanding
Less holed up
in my own little trove of broken things
Maybe if I stopped always making it about me
I owed you that
And I'm learning
I cannot change what is done
Only take you with me forever
and be the one I should have been for you
Maybe I'll never delete your number
Who could fault me for that?

Alive

Waited just long enough to watch the foundations
crumble

Indifferent as it burns to the ground
this empire that once thrived, rich with life

Alas, nothing lasts forever
With the embers still hot among the blackened rubble
Turn away

Continue on in the struggle to find yourself
To grasp meaning
To make your mark
And never return

Fill the void with dangerous vices
Those that make you feel once again
Or those that offer numbness
to this sickening self-indulgent torment

You thrive in the chaos
The anguish, it gives birth to your best work

That sweet taste of bitter denial on your tongue
reminds you that you're alive
and you so long to be alive

Jigsaw

This one there
No, that one here
Wait, that's not right
Pieces spread about
No method to the madness
No order to the chaos
Starting from the middle
Working outward

Unable to see the bigger picture
Forced to learn the hard way
A small chunk put together over here
But no idea where it fits
Another over there
Still doesn't seem to make any sense

Oh, been lookin' for that piece
That goes right there
And this one right here
Now completes another portion

Sitting for hours at a time
Staring at the indistinguishable scenes
On each odd little shape
Trying to make them fit
Turning this way and that
Moving pieces from here to there and back
Go about your day-to-day life
The fulfillment of want & need
It will still be waiting when you return
Haunting you
Begging to be finished
Pining to reveal its secrets

Self-Inflicted

Beautiful little masochist
Filled your head
with the thoughts that mar your soul
Bleeding from the depths
in which you've plunged your own knife
Lay blame on this and that
on anything lying beyond the veil
of your ignorance

Innocent little martyr
Created a waking nightmare
written in your own lies
Wearing your mask of victim
to cover the crippling shame
Breathe life into the disillusion
into the fire you secretly desire

Clever little manipulator
Spread your poison
through an already neglected foundation
Severing lifelong connections
from which you've only received love
Give courtesy to the madness
to the torment you can no longer survive without

The F Word

Falling like flies
The fickle flames of friendship
Frivolous flirtations
found no longer fitting
Flawed, fractured feelings
fill faded pages of former fantasies
While failed foresight gives way to folly
Wave farewell to formidable foes
and fancy fabrications
Fair faces of duality feign fidelity
feeding fallacies of freedom and choice
Forget the fierce flippancy
of foolish fiends
and dare to foster a future unfettered
by such familiar futility

Avarice

Little broken pieces of compulsion
Jagged shards of craving
embedded deep in the scars
that harsh winters of passion left behind
The liars, the cheats
the most heartless of thieves
wickedly weaved an intricate lie of inadequacy
Now, it's all too much
and it's never quite enough
Grieve in the freedom of solitude
Find vanity within the folds of insecurity
Demand more than can be given
Yet ask for less than is deserved
Make madness of the sense
as the addiction calls for another round on the house
and another *I shouldn't* is whispered by the voice that no one hears
Some habits are excruciatingly simple to break
Those self-inflicted controlled burns to purge reality from life,
yet they are the favored vices
of kings & peasants alike

Lunacy

What is this lunacy?
This repetitive need to lay waste to purity
To take what was once so alluring
and level it with calculated misery

Why does it consume?
Building upon a self-induced gloom
Creating a creature riddled with doubt
and a path once promising leads to certain doom

When will it expire?
Such a complex & unyielding desire
Always craving a shrouded sense of calm
while dancing dangerously close to the edge of this fire

Embrace & Endure

Fade from the land slowly as sun gives way to moon
Another cycle lies behind
Another day laid to rest
And again the tide changes
The universe shifts

The great transfiguration
Take just a moment to lean on the goddess for guidance
for reassurance
Then take this metamorphosis
And own it

Create
Strive
Fuel the light
Suffocate the drowning absence
Treading water is for the faint of heart
The scarce of courage
Do not wait for rescue
Exerting against the current is for the ignorant
The foolish
Do not become sick with defiance
Roll with the waves
Surrender to the ebb & flow
Allow them to rejuvenate a soul grown stagnant

And wherever your feet touch the shore
give thanks for the blessed journey
For the opportunity to sew new seeds in fresh soil

You are always home

Moving Mountains

Masterfully masked misery
and myriads of misused moments
mar the surface of a moonlit soul
Yet mystery mingles beneath the madness
and magic melds with the melancholy
A mangled morass of mistakes makes way
for a more meaningful memoir
The mirage melts
Mirth replaces mourning
Mindless mistrust lies in mending
This mauled mortal finds mercy from torment
that mouthwatering masochism of manic self-
mutilation

Such Is Life

Wasted moments of a journey
now decades in the making
Etching lines once faint & few
deeper into the surfaces
of a well-weathered soul
Master the art of self-destruction
with a vice for every occasion
Before reaching such enlightened heights
of true understanding
and the filthy depths
of life-altering awareness
Take these trials
this anguish and the strife
these invisible bonds
Constricting
Restricting
Cast them away
as would a fisherman
with his handmade net
to capture sustenance
in the ebb & flow for which he lives

And So, I Write

Darkness settles in...

The air still,
heavy & thick
surrounding me in a dry, stale heat

Drag after drag I ponder,
lost in meaningless thought

My mind searches my heart
My heart searches my soul
listening for the reason,
yet hearing only silence

Sifting through the debris
for pieces that will once again make me whole

Understanding the need for chaos,
But desperately seeking order

I sit alone,
facing that which I had feared the most
Doubts bear down upon me,
weighing heavily on my shoulders

A risk worth taking & chance to begin a new chapter,
yet ever apprehensive of the unforeseen

This life is mine,
no longer belonging to the demons
nor the fear that had been holding me back

And so I write...

Aware & Enlightened

And now we reach the final stage of this journey - Awareness & Enlightenment. In these pages, we explore the pieces of my identity that I have found along the way, and the concepts which now define my whole self. I have stepped into a new era of my life, and each of these poems showcase how everything that has come before has led to where I am now. I have accepted every facet of who I am, proudly and unabashedly, while understanding that I still have so much more of myself to unlock. It is a lifelong process, but it's important to look back on all the lessons to appreciate how far you have come.

Dear Brother

Drowning slowly in high tides
Gasping for just a hint of air
Not a thought inside my head
Except that no one can save me now

Disappearing into the blackness I've created
Crying aloud, but nobody hears
Desperate for someone to understand
Yet there is no reply

Those who knew me before
Have long since been lost and forgotten
Years of torment have boarded me up
I have lost the reason to love

Suddenly, I feel a gentle hand
Holding me, pulling me from the wreckage
I no longer struggle to breathe
I only patiently wait for the surface

I reach the top and slowly take a breath
As if I've been reborn anew
I open my eyes to gaze upon my savior
And there you are...again

Dear Sister

You are the wish I made on every shooting star
and the dream I never believed would come true
I will forever be an anchor when the sea becomes too harsh
As the storms rage on, I shall be your shelter
The voice of reason in your reckless abandon
Here to defend in every battle against your demons
I shall give you wings to carry your dreams to the stars
And help you find the answers
to the questions that plague your soul with regret
You will never be alone
You will never have to navigate the darkness
Without a light to guide the way
This is my promise to you

Unaffected

To be 17 again
The whole world at my feet
A future so promising
birthed of a past painted in tenebrosity
To be so ignorant again
even in all I'd seen
So blinded to the truly evil ways of wicked men
Still carving an expected place for myself
A cozy little corner that I could call my own
Put up my little picket fence
Plant my garden of flaccid daydreams
Wear my apron proudly
like an obedient little lady created of their colorful lies
laced with romanticized propaganda
To be so certain again
Believing the best laid plans of fairy tales
Writing my own in droves of unbridled reverence
for things I never really understood
Throw caution to the wind
no morsels of my soul devoured by dissonance
The lack of experience overshadowed by illusions
Oh, but to have those illusions again

Fond Affinity

Old habits die hard
.or so they say
I say it's the new more reluctant to loosen its grip
Those fresh experiences that leave you begging for
another round
Richer flavors, deeper understandings
Old habits more often become recognized, called out
They become routine
Bland, uninspired
and give in to the resignation of letting go
But those tasty little morsels of virgin vices
grab attention with fierce domination
and before long you're toeing the dangerous line
of want versus need
Why else would new habits become the old?
Then one day,
you find yourself staring down the barrel
of a proclivity you've justified to a bloody pulp
and buried beneath blind rationalization
If you had just said no after the first nibble
you'd only have a silly campfire story
instead of a tormenting history
But I must admit
When I feel that tender touch upon my skin
by fingertip, eye or lip
Of all my tendencies, both new & old
my addictions both sustained & broken
this new one here
will always be my favorite

Identity

Seems such a silly thing
such an unnecessary irritation

Yet these little relics of long-lost men
who knew not of your pain
and those broken souls
who demanded that which they could not return
hang upon your identity
like weights of the estranged

You wish only to cast them off
to no longer wear the chains shackled by blood
and the bad decisions of your past selves

You wish only to be a character of your own design
instead of the design by those who've misperceived you

What's in a name?
A past of abandonment
A history of deprivation
A battle of self-reliance

All these tokens of possession
you yearn to no longer bear

Resolute

However restless
Whatever the cost
There is acceptance
That it comes

It doesn't come easy
But it comes
It doesn't come cheap
But it comes

With struggle
With longing
With pain
With hardship
With difficulty
It still comes

A train carrying a lonely passenger
Staring out the window
As the time passes
Achingly slow
Yet, it comes

Each track laid
For but one singular purpose
One tedious journey
On its own schedule
Surely it comes

Even as it appears
That these tracks
Will see no end
There is a station where destiny awaits

Built for one arrival
And sure as the sun
Blankets the world in warmth
It comes...

She's Got A Way

Standing tall as the chaos surrounds
She wears her pride like a badge of honor
Holds her head as high as the gods
Survivor, they call her
Hero, they ask of her
She walks the line of give & take
Forever fearing the fall to one side or the other
In her moments of solitude
She weeps
For the broken souls
For the damaged hearts
For those she cannot save
For herself
Men see her grace and crave her touch
They trip over each other
Clamoring for a bit of attention
They throw expectations onto her shoulders
And weigh her down with need
She has spent so long living to please
Now knowing no other way
She is salvation
She is redemption
And yet she seeks only respite
She desires only balance
Longing to lock herself away
To keep herself guarded from those wanting hands
Those demanding egos
Yet, this is her gift
This is her curse
The torch she shall eternally bear

I Am Contradiction

The shadow of love
The light of hate
The difference between fantasy & reality

The ignorance of mature
The wisdom of youth
The distance between freedom & captivity

The brighter side of hell
The darker side of heaven
The muddled line between right & wrong

The honesty of fiction
The deceit of fact
The conflict between weak & strong

The sadness of beauty
The rapture of grotesque
The void between sleep & awake

The mourning of life
The celebration of death
The friction between give & take

Gift & Curse

I write to grow, to remember
to uncover the secrets my mistakes whisper from the pages
Listening to the ink tell a story
and finding within the folds every lesson I dared to learn

Betrayed
Denied
Given less
Taken more
Madly in love
and deeply lost

Inspiration lurks in dimly lit bars
and crowded stadiums
Ensnared
Entranced
Unnumbered lines of teenage angst washed away
in the wake of a hurricane named Experience

Between the seemingly endless rants
of pain
of lust
of pleasure
of loss
of every 'poor little me'
lies true salvation

Tits & Ass

Such a pretty little face
Don't you see?
Nothing that you are really matters
when they have no use
of anything but
eyes and appendages
Worry not for the layers
you yearn to be penetrated
you're going about it all wrong
Don't you know?
Nothing that you offer means more
than the body
they crave to traverse
the lips they desire to defile
Such a simple truth
yet you refuse to accept its bitter taste
Don't you want?
Nothing that you can't manifest
from the game
so well played
by those who understand the rules
But you've never really been one
For fitting into that mold
Have you?

I Never Knew

I had begun to believe this was it
All I've gotten is all I'll ever get
I had created a lie to hide deep within
A dream now fading into history

Because there is more
The wants & needs I have been neglecting
are forcing to the surface
and I know that I can have them all

I have settled
I have chosen to ignore every broken sign
I have given too much
and have so little to show

It is time
To move forward
to journey past this regret
and find my place among the stars

Truth, Reflected

A mirror
A looking glass for all your broken pieces
Reflecting back the wounds you've yet to heal
The darkness you've chosen to deny

The Grief
The Despair
The Insecurity
The Emotional Decay

Gliding in on enigmatic wings
This fatal fantasy you contrived
Cracks you open bit by bit
With tendrils of starlight and whispers of reverie

You invited this echo
You begged for this revelation
You starved yourself for a taste of this judgement
And expected it to oblige your misguided craving
Yet, when it stood before you
Bare, battered, bleeding from the wreckage
When it manifested the truth of yourself
Betraying the lies you weave into your soul
You demanded it adjust its perception

"No more!" you cried
"Let me see myself as I hope to be!"
"I cannot," it replied
"You will only ever see what you truly are in me..."

Incongruous

A scrap of brilliant silk among envious shards of broken glass
The breath of light illuminating despite suffocating darkness
Unpretentious in a world so dangerously crass
Guided by empathy along raging waves of the heartless

Weaving threads of wisdom from a tapestry of willful ignorance
A canvas of daring colors stark against the safety of black and white
Lyrical harmony beyond the cacophony of dissonance
Wearing imperfection proudly despite the illusion of unmarred sight

A tree of oak everlasting in this throw away culture
This flame of ferocity that burns through a landscape painted bleak
Wide awake as these blinded masses revel in their slumber
A voice loud and defiant amid the chorus of the meek

Balance

A favored idea, Balance
A hopeful desire for everything in its right place
Most pray for only peace
Such a noble, yet misguided dream
Without the balance of chaos
the very experience of strife
Without the darkness of pain
One would never come to know the strength of overcoming
Nor the light of forgiveness and release
We would not evolve
We would become stagnant
Unchanging
What is the point of a life left unlived?
No, do not wish for only peace
Wish for balance
Dream of fluidity between the storms
Focus on beauty while acknowledging the existence of grotesque
I wonder why so few share in my pursuit
Perhaps I ask too much
Perhaps my perspective blinds me to the demands
or perhaps I spent so long bending for the sake of others
that I have become deeply selfish
I have yet to fully unravel the truth at the core of those needs
but I will not stop fighting for my place
I will overcome

The Undoing

The mask falls
The illusion distorts
As this reality changes form once again
The mold breaks
The one never meant to hold you
And the undoing begins

Too long, too many false faces
Ripping away the faded pages
Rewriting the story
With a quill dipped in the blood
Of ancestors long silenced
And the rage of all their buried suffering

Reshape
Rearrange
Rediscover
Scream into the void
Of who you were supposed to be
As who you were always meant to be
Claws its way to the surface

No more appeasing
The whims of those
Who would see you shrink
Afraid of your muchness
Of your power, your voice
Of the flame that only an existence
Such as yours could ignite

Never Call Me Indifferent

Indifferent?
Never

The depth of all this empathy cannot be reached
The weight of all this suffering cannot be quantified
The grief of all this dissonance cannot be fathomed

Never Indifferent

When I say "I feel"
I mean that my very bones ache with an undeniable longing
to express the ways in which I internalize your wounds

When I say "I understand"
I mean that every fiber of my being knows without question
the battles you speak of and yearns to absorb their heaviness

When I say "I am here"
I mean that even as I struggle to carry my own demons
there are no ends to which I wouldn't go to help you carry yours

When I say "I love"
I mean that my entire existence is spent pouring my light

into every soul that is brave enough to share their heart
with me

Yet, the point of utter exhaustion has long since passed
The anguish of giving only to be wrung so painfully dry
has taken a toll I can no longer deny
The juxtaposition of holding a million candles
only to drown in unrelenting darkness
has burned all the inclination to constantly be your
saviour

I am not indifferent
I still grasp firmly the multitudes in each life of which
my path crosses
wrapping them around my very core
cradling them with a reverence few will ever
comprehend

But I will not bury my own desires for your comfort
nor will I shoulder the responsibility for every
misfortune that befalls you
You are welcome to cast me as your villain
and I will play my part with feverish delight

But never call me indifferent

Stretch

Muscles, tense with apprehension
slowly uncoil
and new breath tickles the senses
Relief swirls within the veins
of a body renewed
Full of accomplishment
Full of pride
Yet those pale in comparison
to the peace that comes with knowing
Everything in its right place
Work still to be done
Mistakes yet to be learned from
There will always be darkness
some unexpected disharmony that dares to vie for control
My glow will burn brighter
With feet planted more firmly
and resolve pushing even further
Standing at the ready
A queen surveying the kingdom she has built
brick by bloody brick
and an army of warriors at my back,
souls the very definition of everlasting
I will not be underestimated
Fate, do your worst

Resistance

They bend you
crack you
Hold you tight
Using your light
to illuminate their darkness
And then discard you
as it begins to dim
Because you can't shine
all the time
You can't give and give until the well is dry
You can't be all they need
while neglecting yourself

They hate you for it
for not staying
for not enduring
for not placating
For daring to believe
that your worth is more
than what you can provide
in service to others

And when your true fire burns?
When you have taken every broken splinter
every cheap token of adoration
from every lying grifter
to use as kindling
in the blaze that will bring down
this hollow facade of who they

expected you to be...

They call you selfish
Too loud
Too proud
Too real
Too raw
A complication which refused
this blatant exploitation
A useless mess in a tattered dress
Who would want such a defiant possession?

And to them, I say...
Who would ever want to be possessed
by a heart with such ill intentions?
By a soul with such shallow pretensions?
By hands wringing with lust to only lay claim
over that which they never deserved?

You will never again feel the magic
that lies beneath my skin
or taste the desire that wrapped you in decadent sin
And as your existence fades into obscurity
You will never forget my name
nor the price you paid in your futile quest
to brand me as your villain

Fear

Such a natural emotion to fall prey to,
Fear
It stiffens your very soul, makes weeping children of your judgment and intuition
Tears at your courage and causes you to rethink all of your choices

Such a fickle friend, fear
Cradles you in comfortable apathy
But steep too long in those doubts and you shall surely rot from the inside out

Am I afraid?
Of course I am

Afraid that the pride I've tasted only in brief, fleeting moments will again place itself just out of my reach
Afraid that my resolve will wash away like countless dreams with the morning rain
Afraid I will once again fall victim to the destructive patterns into which I so eagerly slide

Afraid that all the
Dedication
Exploration
Calculation
Perspiration
it took to anchor myself will have been for naught

Yes, I am afraid

But if you’ve never felt it, then you've not truly lived a moment

It is only when you allow that fear to steer your course
that your mistakes become cyclical
I want nothing more than to indulge the convenience of my anxieties
and let worry take the wheel
Yet, I will not

I am the very definition of strength and conviction
From my first steps on this Earth I have been paving my own road, which you can see littered with the expectations I could not meet and the demands I refused to fulfill
I will not give in to incertitude
I will not be dominated, moderated, regulated or suffocated

I will fight for what has always been mine to hold
the story that is mine to unfold
the existence that is mine to mold
And I will carry within me the spirits of my matriarchy as I create this stunning new reality
from the darkness that beckons my soul
and the fear that I will control

A Short Story in Progress

These next few pages are a short story I have been working on for the better part of two decades. It all started with a writing prompt competition in my college days – 1,000 words or less using ten words that were provided. I don't know if any of those remain, but it inspired this constantly evolving piece that may yet become a full-fledged novel. For now, it will be something I continue to work on, refine, add to, subtract from...but I wanted to end this book with it because of how it has grown with me over the years. The original story is still weaved within the first few pages, but even that has changed, much like me. So, enjoy, and thank you for joining me on this journey...I hope you learned something, felt something, and connected with at least one piece along the way.

The Last Taste

The rain had stopped for the first time in days, but left its essence in dark, glistening pools that littered the abandoned street. Grey clouds hung low in the sky as they threatened another downpour. The bare trees that lined the road dripped and had already begun to frost over in the bone-chilling cold that swept through the air. It was dusk, although the sun was nowhere to be found, and the loneliness of night began to drape itself across the city. Bethany pulled her jacket even tighter around her body as she continued on, wishing class had ended an hour earlier. The wind whipped around her, biting her nose and stinging her eyes. She sloshed through another deep puddle, determined to make it home before it was utterly black on the unlit streets of her neighborhood.

Suddenly, she felt that familiar presence in the coming darkness; that feeling of being watched by covetous eyes in those moments when she was alone. Its omnipresence was at times suffocating, a desire for dangerous interludes that would float in on the wind and swim deep within her own madness, begging her to simply give in to its advances. Even as she hungered for the interaction this creature could grant her, the fear welled up inside her throat and she began to quicken her pace. Her heartbeat became erratic, her temperature rising as her limbs began to shake from something other than the cold. She quickened to a run even though she was not more than a few hundred feet from her building. As she ran, she felt the eyes fading into the shadows, as if it were playing with her, allowing her to get away.

She hit the stairs up to her apartment without a single glance back and fumbled for the key in her jacket pocket. She ignored the notice on her door that hadn't been there this morning as she turned the key, rushed inside, and slammed it behind her. Inside the warm, safe confines of her front hall, she locked the deadbolt, stripped the jacket from her body and kicked off her drenched sneakers. The water and mud that splattered the white tile floor as she did was of no concern at the present moment. Tomorrow, she would deal with it. Leaning against the wall, she shuddered at the thought of what could be watching her so intently. Yet, the elation of such a thought stirred her curiosity in a way that she had never felt. Sighing, she began to undress as she walked through her apartment, dropping pieces of clothing on the salmon-colored carpet, tossing them on the ugly blue couch that had been given to her by her last neighbor, and on the four-poster canopy bed made of rich, dark cherry wood. Grabbing a few of her favorite gardenia candles off the dresser, she made her way to the bathroom and drew a hot bubble bath to calm her nerves and warm her blood. She detested the cold, had her whole life, and couldn't imagine how anything had convinced her to move to Washington, where it was cold and rainy for more than half the year. *'Fucking Jeremiah,'* she thought.

Just over a year ago, she had packed up everything she could fit in her truck to drive from warm, sunny southern California to the dreary streets of West Queen Anne outside Seattle. Her fiancé had moved there a few months prior with his band to pursue a "career" in music, and she had soon followed. She had given up school, a great job, friends, and family to support him in his decision. She had gone against the pleas and warnings of those she loved most to be with the man she was going to marry. And that choice had exiled her from all she had ever known. She got a job as a waitress at a local mom-and-pop joint not far from the house they had shared with his three buddies, and did portrait and event photography on the side to pay the bills while Jeremiah and his band, *Branded*, struggled with small gigs around the city. After seven months of failing to make a name for himself there, Jeremiah disappeared. Without a word to let her know where he'd gone, Bethany came home after a long night at the restaurant to a half-empty house and a pile of unpaid bills.

As she sank into the steaming water and rested her head on a bath pillow, the memories of pain trickled from her eyes. He had left her, abandoned her in loneliness to chase dreams he would never grasp. She had not believed it in the beginning. She had told herself that he would come back, that he loved her. She was his muse, his reason for existence...he had told her so not days before he vanished. Then, about two months after his sudden departure, the permanence of his absence set in. She had yet to come to terms with it, but knew that she had to move on. So she had found an apartment of her own, began taking night classes at the community college, got herself a beautiful little black cat with large green eyes to keep her company, and immersed her life in work. She longed for some sort of companionship...a friend, a weekend lover, anything to chase away the feeling of emptiness that consumed her.

She closed her eyes and let the sadness escape for a while. After more than an hour, she felt that terrifying and thrilling presence weighing down upon her again. Sitting up quickly, sloshing water over the side of the tub, she scanned the room for any clue, any reason why her mind could be playing such tricks on her. There was nothing. She climbed out of the bath, grabbed her worn black robe, and headed slowly for the bedroom. Dinah was sprawled at the foot of the bed, almost invisible against the midnight blue bedspread as she meowed at Bethany's entrance hoping for a bit of affection. Not a thing was out of place, not even the cat seemed to notice anything out of the ordinary, yet she couldn't shudder off the feeling - she knew he was out there.

It had been going on for months now, since just after she'd moved into her apartment & started taking classes. She'd considered classmates, but none of them really seemed the type – not that she really knew much about them, except what little bits she learned from their assignments. And none of her regular customers at work stood out much either, but in a restaurant environment, especially one as busy as this often gets, it's hard to notice such things. It wasn't like she got gifts or cards, or even creepy phone calls either...he was just always watching her, admiring her from afar. She couldn't bring herself to call it stalking, that word sounded wrong when she thought about it. Her conflicted feelings about the whole thing were driving her mad. She had to find out who he was...and more importantly, what he wanted.

***

He remembered the first time he saw her, at Kinnear Park not far from his townhouse, the tastes of autumn on the breeze. She looked magnificent in her blue sweater & jeans, long hair the shade of dark chocolate, and a camera hiding most of her face. She was busy snapping away at foliage changing for the season and children chasing a golden Labrador around beneath the trees. She was so intent, so lost in the magic of what she could see through that lens, and he'd never seen something so breathtakingly perfect in all his years. While he watched her capture a trove of wonders he couldn't know, never fully seeing her face, he followed her path through the park for the better part of an hour. He was instantly enamored. At one point she turned his direction about forty feet ahead of him, the barrel of her microscope aimed directly at him, and he could swear he heard the faint shutter click as she immortalized him in a single moment before continuing on to his left. The question of whether or not she truly saw him standing there - whether or not she went home and stared at that photo the way he gazed upon her - burned constantly inside his head.

After that beautiful morning, he started haunting all the places he thought a woman like her would want to capture, hoping to see her again. It didn't take long; Queen Anne is a fairly small town. He stumbled across her a little over a week later at the Mount Pleasant cemetery. There she was, this time in a red pea coat and matching knit cap stark against the gray tones of the overcast evening, gliding effortlessly among the grave stones on her photographic mission. He followed her again for a short time trying to catch a glimpse of what he was sure was an angelic face. Once, he lost her among the large crypts that nestled closely to a grove of Magnolia trees. He was caught by surprise when she came around a rather large tomb right in his path, nearly bumping into him. In a split second, he was looking into the most stunning sea green eyes framed by a thick set of lashes and complimenting fair, nearly porcelain skin. She smiled just a bit with perfectly formed pink lips, the hint of a dimple in her left cheek. This was a face far more lovely than he had imagined...and he was struck completely silent. He knew it was awkward, the way he stood there just staring at her, but he couldn't force himself to shatter the moment with words.

"I didn't mean to interrupt your mourning," she purred with a voice like soft rain on a slow Sunday afternoon, "but I was wondering if I could take your picture. I'm working on a project for school, and I need to work in a human element." She smiled again, with only the slightest show of teeth and a bold look in her soulful eyes. She fidgeted with her camera then, taking those eyes off of him momentarily, and he finally remembered to breathe. After a few moments, she looked back up expectantly – then he realized she'd asked him a question.

"That's okay, I'm sorry again for intruding," she said with a slight frown and started away back down the path. He panicked, not wanting her to leave, but unable to form a solid thought.

"Wait…" he finally sputtered out. She turned back, and he was afraid if she looked at him directly again, he wouldn't be able to answer her, so he glanced up at the grand memorial next to him and simply said, "…sure." He heard a few clicks in succession and looked back at her as the camera came down from in front of her smiling face.

"Thanks. I know it's strange, photographing shrines to the dead, but I'm kind of fascinated by cemeteries. The whole idea of visiting the graves of those souls who are no longer anchored here…it's like our personal brand of torture, our inability to let go manifested by the justification of honoring another's life after death." She stopped, perhaps realizing this was not the conversation to be having with someone standing at a grave site. "Oh man, I'm so rude…I'm sure that's not something you want to hear right now. Sorry for your loss." And again, she turned to leave.

"No, no...it's fine, really. I'm not visiting anyone here," he throws out before he loses her, "I'm just, uh, taking a walk."

"In a cemetery? Well, at least I know I don't appear that strange then," she said with a light laugh. He could have listened to her talk & laugh like that for hours. He finally smiled back, elated that he found some way to connect with this alluring creature.

"Not at all. I agree with you...I'd never want to be buried like this. I don't want to think of loved ones returning to their pain week after week. I'd want to be honored by them living their lives & celebrating what mine stood for, what I'd accomplished with the time I was given."

"Exactly. Glad I'm not the only one. It was a pleasure to meet you...and thank you again for being my momentary model. I've got to get to work."

"Oh, um, yeah...okay. I'm...Nicholas, by the way. The pleasure was entirely mine," he stammered. He really wanted to put a name to this lovely woman.

"Bethany," she said, again with that little smile, "maybe we'll see each other again somewhere." With that she finally left him standing there in silence, dumbstruck that this exchange of common ideas had even occurred.

'Bethany,' he thought to himself, *'I surely intend to see you again.'*

***

After she finished her double shift at T. S. McHugh's, quite a fruitful day as she ended up with nearly $250 in tips, she got a ride from the dishwasher Marty who lived a couple blocks over from her and refused to allow her to walk home on these late evenings. He was always such a gentleman; at one point she'd considered him in her list of suspected admirers, but she later found out he was happily married and a father of three, not at all interested in her as anything other than a friendly coworker. She was actually relieved to hear that; the thought of it being Marty seemed almost boring. No, this man had to be something...intriguing – she imagined more of a charming, wickedly handsome man, with fire in his eyes and an intimidating presence. He wasn't hiding because he feared confronting her. No, he was simply fascinated with watching her, the way she moved and carried herself. He would make his move sooner rather than later.

She went back through her ever-shrinking list of suspects, trying to pin one of them down as more probable than the others. There was Enson, the quiet & intense owner of the bookstore she frequented. He was always staring at her, though she rarely caught him in the act – she could feel the way he looked at her. Jesse, with whom she'd had a cup of coffee after he'd helped her in the Photography lab at school – he was in other classes & just happened to be there while she was working on an assignment. She hadn't seen him but in passing between classes or in the parking lot after that, and he always seemed to have a genuine smile for her. Last, there was Marcus with his easy smile and dancing eyes. Marcus was the only friend who'd remained after Jeramiah left, the only one who had seen how it devastated her and been a comfort to her, although somewhat distantly. They weren't close by any means, he'd simply come around every so often to grab a bite and maybe catch a movie with her, get her out of the house. Other than her studies and work, she pretty much stayed in. He'd never hinted at anything romantic, but there was something about the way he held her when they embraced after every innocent rendezvous that was charged with a well-hidden longing. Yet, all of them had ample opportunity to make such feelings known. Bethany had never been repulsed by or uninterested in any of them, so why hadn't they come forward? There had to be someone else.

Her thoughts took an interesting turn then, as she sifted through the last four or five months for anyone she may have left out, and ended up back on an accidental and brief meeting with that stranger at the cemetery a few months ago. She had his picture somewhere. Odd she would think of that now...she got an A on the project she'd been working on all based on that photo but hadn't given it much thought afterwards. She had captured something memorable, something poetic, and her teacher had loved it. Hadn't he looked familiar that day? She switched on her computer and poured a cup of tea, opening first those project photos. She found the shot of him; a long, dark overcoat hung on his frame perfectly, as if it were tailored; short, dark hair and an impressive profile that featured his excellent bone structure as he stared up into the cold eyes of the Angel of Death statue before him. It was a very beautiful shot - even though he had not known the soul buried there it was as if he were momentarily channeling some great love of this long-dead life, like they were seeing this grave through his eyes and reminiscing. She couldn't place it, but she knew she'd seen this face before.

With renewed vigor to find the mysterious entity which followed her, she began pouring through her files, starting with school projects and then making her way to the personal shots. It took her the better part of two hours to hunt him down, but she found him again. Not once, but at least half a dozen times. The first shot of him had been just after she'd moved to her new place, when she went for her first walk in Kinnear Park about two miles from her apartment building. The leaves had just started changing, the overcast sky had given way to sunshine, and there were a few moms with their kids and dogs out at the park that day. It had instantly become her favorite place to get lost with her camera; there was always something worth shooting - families gathered for picnics and small sporting events with the kids; lovers walking hand in hand down the many hidden paths; a variety of animals & birds; she'd even managed to capture a few shots of an intimate wedding ceremony once. And he had been there, this beautiful shadow that never dared to purposefully get close to her. He was standing beneath a large Maple tree, looking right at her and she'd never noticed...she was taking in the whole scene with the small pond behind him and the sun just dipping behind the trees – the golden hour, they called it, was a favored shooting time. It was almost as if she had caught him by surprise. In fact, all the photos she found with him were the same, with the exception of the one in the cemetery. He was partially hidden, staring at her, and totally unprepared to be in her line of sight.

Down at the harbor, he leaned against a docked schooner of white and red, wrapped in the same coat with that somewhat startled look on his face. At the Chihuly Garden & Glass Museum she found him in one of the darker galleries, standing as if he were inspecting one of the bright sculptures she was trying to capture, but he was again looking right at her, his face illuminated by the display light while the rest of him was shrouded in darkness. These encounters weren't evenly spaced out either, as if by some strange coincidence he just happened to be there but were randomly spread...it had been almost two weeks between the cemetery & harbor visits, and over a month before she hit the museum. How many other times had he been there that she hadn't managed to catch him?

She racked her brain now for the specifics of that exchange of words they had shared. What had he said then? Something about just going for a walk...and his name! He'd told her his name! What the fuck was it?! Benjamin? Alexander? No, she knew it at least started with an 'N'. Nathaniel? Noel? Dammit...it was on the tip of her tongue. She glanced at the clock then and cursed out loud...it was three in the morning, and she had an interview with the local paper in five hours for a freelance photographer position. She shut down her computer and crawled into bed; her thoughts still focused on the stranger and his piercing gray eyes akin to swirling storm clouds.

***

He had been watching her for months and now knew her patterns – the paths she took between home, work and school, her favorite spots to walk with her camera, the little bookstore where she'd spend hours hunting for a myriad of titles, the coffee shop at which all the employees knew her usual order and table as she feverishly attacked a notebook with unknown thoughts. He knew her favorite color as he nearly always saw her dressed in some shade of blue; he knew she didn't have any family or close friends, at least none here, as she never met up with anyone personally or went to others' homes; he knew she adored the changing seasons, flowers, animals & children – those were all her favorite things to capture; he knew she especially loved white flowers, as he caught the lovely scent of gardenia & jasmine when he was near her; he knew she had a black cat she loved fiercely, but was otherwise alone in this often rainy and dark little town. Yes, he knew her. Yet, there was so much more he longed to find.

Why was she here, alone? He had been in Queen Anne for most of his exceptionally long life; he and his mother had fled here, their little hiding place in the northwest corner of the country as far from New Orleans and her many sins as they could get. He knew everyone in town, aside from the random tourist who stayed for only a month or so to escape reality, and he'd never seen Bethany before. What was her story; where did she come from? He was more than intrigued...he was fascinated to such a degree he knew it bordered stalking. He wanted to know the feel of her skin, the taste of her lips, the depth of her desires. He wanted to unwrap her deepest pains and uncover every facet of her life; he needed to know everything; he simply couldn't let it go.

Oftentimes he found himself wondering if she knew he was even there, if she had seen him in those photos she had taken where he stood in the shadows. And if she did, was she frightened...or excited? As he waited for her to come around the corner, headed for the Cederberg Tea House on her usual Saturday afternoon visit, the thought crossed his mind that she was completely oblivious to his presence. That worried him – he'd rather her be scared than ignorant. He wanted her to know, to wonder, to ponder. He hoped that she knew when she bolted to her apartment a few weeks back that he didn't mean her harm, which is why he hadn't immediately followed. Of course, he had eventually…and had nearly decided it was time to confront this beast of longing. Yet, some small part of him feared that she wouldn't be what he saw in her. He would have played her up, created this fantasy of denial and when he tasted her, he would find himself sorely disappointed. He feared she would let him down, like they all did.

He had hesitated long enough to leave it be. Funny, prior to that moment, he'd felt no fear of revealing himself to her. This elated him in ways he couldn't describe. This was something new for him. He'd never placed any of them on this high a pedestal; he'd always believed they'd never live up so he'd never given himself a moment of false hope. Bethany was something else entirely and the thought of her laying perfectly bare before him actually scared the shit out of him the more he ran through it in his mind. It also got him strangely aroused.

So, there he stood, like some creep in the bushes with a raging hard-on waiting for some unknowing victim, who was now late. She was rarely late…if anything, she was habitually early to a fault. The erection faltered as he realized she wasn't coming. She never missed her Saturday ritual, not once in the last five months. Now he was really worried and had no idea what to do about it. If he started actively checking her apartment and work, he could run the risk of being seriously exposed, and he knew he wasn't quite ready for that. There was no use waiting here any longer, so he decided to just head home, the one place he never wanted to be.

***

Bethany made her way to the café, pleased with the way her interview went. It would be a few days before she heard back, but she was confident.

"Good afternoon, Beth, we missed you this morning." She was greeted with a friendly smile by Rosie, the manager at Cederberg. "The usual then?" Rosie asked as she started prepping the berry tea that Bethany so loved.

"Hey Rosie, good to see you. No tea today, I need a strong dose of caffeine, what have you got?"

"Our house blend coffee is good & strong; I can add some vanilla & cinnamon if you'd like. Your table is open; I'll bring it over in a few."

"Sounds perfect, thanks."

Bethany headed outside to her favorite spot on the sidewalk, where she had a great view of the little park and shops across the street. She sat down with her journal and before she knew it, she was painting a beautiful, dark picture of her mystery admirer with her words. She didn't even notice when Rosie brought her drink along with a couple warm buttered croissants. She still couldn't remember his name, and the little sleep she had gotten was riddled with sharp images of his stormy eyes. On her way here, she had found herself looking for him, and sorely disappointed that she never saw him or even felt his presence. What kind of weirdo did that make her? She knew on some level this had to be unhealthy, but she couldn't help herself. It wasn't so much the flattery of being so admired, more the desire to know why he didn't reveal himself after all these months of pining from afar. He didn't appear weak or timid to her, so it couldn't be a fear of rejection. It was driving her mad.

She felt so off now – she wasn't here at her usual time, she couldn't feel him lurking around somewhere nearby, always so well-hidden that she finally stopped trying to home in on him. Suddenly the excitement from the interview waned. She had no one to share it with, and at least he could have been there to celebrate with her, even from the shadows. She found it comforting to know he was there, delighting in her day by day. So where was he now? Had he moved onto something better, someone new? Why waste so many months and then suddenly bail out? She couldn't believe she was on this train of thought. *It's absurd,* she told herself. *Think about it logically for one fucking second, Beth…he's a* stalker. *However, you want to slice it up and justify any of it, that's the bare truth. Stalker. You could be one of any number of girls; he could be dangerous.*

But she couldn't convince herself of that. She had to be the only one. And if he was intent on hurting her surely, he would've made his move by now, he'd had plenty of opportunities. She closed her eyes, focusing on that day in the cemetery; on the heavy aroma of rotting leaves & freshly turned earth peppered with a different kind of death; on his dark features so well complimented by the grey tones of the overcast day; on their awkwardly casual exchange of words about mourning. His eyes were always the crispest detail of the image she painted. Icy gray intensity, as if a blue flame burned just behind them, throwing off sharp reflections of light. They were so utterly distracting; she had to add them in last.

"Beth?" She was ripped from her fantasy by a familiar voice, finding herself staring down at a drawing, those wicked eyes staring back up from the page. She hadn't known she'd be drawing; it had been years since she produced anything this good. She pulled away from the paper to find Jesse with a questioning look on his face.

"Are you okay?" he asked quietly, glancing at the drawing.

"Oh, yeah, fine…sorry, guess I was just really focused," she laughed off his worry, "what's up?"

"Um, nothing. I just saw you sitting here as I was coming out of the print shop and thought I'd say hi." He was wearing his signature smile, a little shy and very endearing. It was probably his best quality.

Beth smiled back, "well, hi. Any new shots to show off?"

"Actually, I do, and I wanted your opinion," he finally said and seemed to ease up. He took the other seat at her table and pulled out his latest photos to show her.

***

Nicholas made his way through the winding streets near the harbor, irritation at his mother once again boiled his blood. She knew exactly what she was doing, this coy bullshit wasn't going to fly anymore, he told himself. He knew she'd been going to the bar, playing the pathetic patrons who frequent the place for free drinks and who knows what else. Who knows what she was really giving in return...or what she was taking. He's always known the real reason they fled his birthplace, and her downright ridiculous story of the events that unfolded so many years ago has fallen from her lips so many times she probably believed it's the truth. Delusional, naïve little Rose, the wilted flower of the Bayou; mommy & daddy couldn't control her and the South couldn't hold her. Got herself mixed up in the wrong things with the wrong people and didn't have a helping hand to turn to. *"Such a common and boring tale,"* he thinks, "*why did I have to come from such uninspired beginnings?"*

He sighed and turned down the last street before reaching one of his spots near the coffee shop, where he could see her perfectly at her table knowing he was hidden well. Hopefully she would be there, simply having gotten caught up elsewhere. He was smart enough to have a few vantage points, so as not to bring any attention to himself. He saw her sitting there and that excitement welled up inside of him, the one he always got when he was so close to her, the masochism created deep within our souls that drives so much of what we do…that unfathomable desire. It quickly turned to anger when he noticed the kid sitting across from her, holding what appeared to be some photos. He has only seen her with someone once before, in the very beginning, when she went out for a few hours with some guy that showed up at her place. They appeared friendly, but nothing more. This kid though, he had his eyes all over her, and they were filled to the brim with lust. Nicholas could see the hopeful longing on his face even from here…surely Bethany had to. Who the fuck was he?! And *what the fuck* was he doing there with her? He realized he was digging his fingers into the concrete retainer wall in front of him, blood already seeping into the porous material as cracks formed in its surface.

"This will *not* do," he said out loud, not a care in his head if anyone passing by overhears him talking to himself, "I can't have him interfering, it will ruin everything."

~ The End…For Now ~

LeAnne Hart is an emerging author in the realm of fantasy literature & poetry, as well as an Editor, whose passion for storytelling ignited at a young age. Her literary pursuits are fueled by an enduring fascination with both the boundless possibilities of imaginative fiction and the profound insights of well-crafted non-fiction. LeAnne's formative years were steeped in the art of language, and she honed her writing prowess through a dedicated study of Journalism and Creative Writing. These disciplines instilled in her a meticulous attention to detail, a commitment to factual accuracy, and the ability to weave compelling narratives that resonate with a variety of readers. Her poetic sensibilities imbue her prose with a lyrical quality, lending an emotional depth and relatability to her storytelling.

Currently residing in Arizona, LeAnne finds inspiration in the vibrant tapestry of her surroundings. Her life is enriched by the companionship of a beloved feline, Laszlo, and a diverse array of interests that nourish her creative spirit. When she is not immersed in the world of words, LeAnne can be found indulging her passions for baking delectable treats, crafting intricate works of art, cultivating a flourishing garden, exploring the boundless world of music, embarking on journeys to new and exciting destinations, and cherishing precious moments with her family and friends.

Her other works also include The Salvation of Cylendri Trilogy – an Epic Fantasy Romance of which Book 1 (Sacri'Sanguis) is currently out and Book 2 is slated for release in 2026!

www.ingramcontent.com/pod-product-compliance
Lightning Source LLC
Chambersburg PA
CBHW060623310726
48982CB00003B/657

* 9 7 9 8 9 9 8 6 4 3 6 2 0 *